'Lying on the cans of food was a crumpled newspaper . . . and slap on the front page was my photograph with a banner headline: ESCAPED SAFE ROBBER STILL FREE.

It wasn't a good photograph, but good enough, and she had pencilled in my moustache on the photograph to tell me that she knew who I was.

In the silence of the safe, clean kitchen, I heard the screams of a man in the punishment cell and the hissing crack of the belts as the guards beat him. I saw again the guy who had lost an eye. . . .

My dream of safety dissolved.'

And convict Chet Carson found himself at the mercy of a beautiful, ruthless woman, who ordered him to open her husband's safe and get her the money – or she'd send him back to jail. But events move fast and Chet soon realises that his only chance of survival is to keep that safe locked!

Also by James Hadley Chase

AN ACE UP MY SLEEVE
JUST ANOTHER SUCKER
I WOULD RATHER STAY POOR
LAY HER AMONG THE LILIES
DOUBLE SHUFFLE
THE GUILTY ARE AFRAID
HAVE A CHANGE OF SCENE
NOT SAFE TO BE FREE
YOU'RE LONELY WHEN YOU'RE DEAD
A LOTUS FOR MISS QUON
THERE'S ALWAYS A PRICE TAG
EVE
KNOCK, KNOCK! WHO'S THERE?
SAFER DEAD
THE WORLD IN MY POCKET
SO WHAT HAPPENS TO ME?
THE WARY TRANSGRESSOR
MAKE THE CORPSE WALK
THE THINGS MEN DO
YOU'VE GOT IT COMING
GOLDFISH HAVE NO HIDING PLACE
THE FLESH OF THE ORCHID
BELIEVE THIS YOU'LL BELIEVE ANYTHING
SHOCK TREATMENT
YOU NEVER KNOW WITH WOMEN
LADY HERE'S YOUR WREATH
MISS SHUMWAY WAVES A WAND
THE JOKER IN THE PACK
BUT A SHORT TIME TO LIVE
NO ORCHIDS FOR MISS BLANDISH
DO ME A FAVOUR — DROP DEAD

and published by Corgi Books

James Hadley Chase

Come Easy – Go Easy

CORGI BOOKS
A DIVISION OF TRANSWORLD PUBLISHERS LTD

COME EASY – GO EASY
A CORGI BOOK 0 552 10616 X

Originally published in Great Britain by
Robert Hale Ltd.

PRINTING HISTORY
Robert Hale edition published 1960
Corgi edition published 1977

Corgi Books are published by Transworld Publishers Ltd.,
Century House, 61–63 Uxbridge Road,
Ealing, London, W.5.
Made and printed in Great Britain by
Hunt Barnard Printing Ltd., Aylesbury, Bucks.

CHAPTER ONE

I

AN emergency call came in at five minutes to eleven, just when I was getting ready to leave. If it had come in five minutes later I could have safely ignored it, but with still five minutes to go before official closing time, I was stuck with it.

The night telephone was hooked to a tape recorder that automatically began recording when the telephone bell rang. It was part of this Big-Brother-is-watching-you efficiency system we have.

I picked up the receiver.

"Lawrence Safes Corporation—night service," I said.

"This is Henry Cooper." One of those well fed, arrogant voices that come out of owners of vast incomes and super-de-luxe penthouses. "How fast can you get a man to me? I'm in trouble with my safe."

I thought: here goes my evening with Janey. This makes the third time this month I've had to stand her up.

"Where are you, sir?" I said, keeping my voice polite because the tape was recording, and I had already been in trouble for snarling at a customer.

"Ashley Arms. I want a man down here right away."

I looked at the clock on the desk. It was two minutes to eleven. If I told him the night service had shut down, I would get the gate. The way I was fixed for money, that was a luxury I couldn't afford.

"Can you tell me what is wrong with the safe, sir?"

"I've mislaid the key. Get a man down here fast!"

He banged down the receiver and I banged down mine.

I had promised Janey I would pick her up at eleven-fifteen. We had planned to go dancing at a club that had recently opened. She would be dressed and waiting. Ashley Arms was at the other side of the town. By the time I got there, opened this goddamn safe, got back and parked the van, taken a trolley to her place it would be half-past twelve. I couldn't imagine Janey waiting for me that long. She had told me the next time I stood her up would be the last.

5

I couldn't telephone her from the office. Private calls weren't allowed. There was a phone booth down the road. I would have to call her from there.

I grabbed my tool kit, locked up and went out to the truck. It was beginning to rain and I hadn't a raincoat. The traffic was heavy and there was nowhere to park when I reached the phone booth. It took me ten minutes circling around before some guy pulled out and I could leave the truck.

It was twenty minutes past eleven when I dialled Janey's number. She answered right away as if she had been sitting by the telephone waiting for me to call up and tell her the date was off.

As soon as I started to explain, she hit the ceiling.

"If you can't come, then I know someone who can," she said. "I warned you, Chet. This is the last time. I'm sick and tired of you breaking dates with me. This is the last time!"

"But Janey, I can't help . . ."

But I was talking on a dead line. She had hung up on me.

I dialled her number again, but she didn't answer. I let the bell ring for a couple of minutes, then I cut the connection and went out to the truck.

To make matters worse, it was now raining fit to drown a duck. I drove over to Ashley Arms in a mood of black depression. I cursed the Lawrence Safes Corporation. I cursed Mr. Henry Cooper and I cursed myself for not bringing a raincoat with me, knowing I would have to walk home after I had taken the truck back to the depot and the rain would ruin my best suit that wasn't much anyway.

Ashley Arms was a big apartment block in the best residential district of the town.

I walked into the lobby and over to the doorman's office. He told me I would find Mr. Cooper's apartment on the third floor.

Henry Cooper was tall and bulky, and very, very arrogant. He had a purple complexion of a heavy drinker and a waist-line of a solid eater. He opened the front door himself, and as soon as I stepped into the hall he began to yell at me for taking so long to get out there.

I said the traffic was bad and I was sorry. This he brushed aside, and still muttering, he led the way into a luxuriously furnished lounge.

He walked over to an oil painting of a fat woman in the nude that looked good enough to be an original Rubens, but probably wasn't, and swung the painting on its hinges aside. Behind it was one of our super-de-luxe wall safes.

As I was setting down my tool kit, I became aware of a girl lying full length on the settee. She was in a white evening dress cut so low I could see the tops of her breasts. She was leafing through a magazine, a cigarette between her full red lips, and she glanced up and stared curiously at me.

She reminded me a little of Janey. She had the same coloured hair and the same long, slender legs, but there the resemblance ended. This girl had a lot of class whereas Janey had no class at all. Janey had a provocative shape, personality and a duck tail walk that made men stare after her, but it was all pretty brash. There was nothing brash about this girl.

"How soon can you open it?" Cooper demanded. "I'm in a hurry."

With a conscious effort I shifted my eyes from the girl and went over to the safe.

"Not long, sir, if you will give me the combination."

He scribbled the combination down on a scrap of paper and gave it to me. Then he went over to the cellarette and began to fix himself a highball.

As I started work on the safe, I heard a telephone bell ring somewhere in the apartment.

"I guess that'll be Jack," Cooper said to the girl and he went out of the room, leaving the door open.

The girl said softly, "Hurry it up, buster. The old stinker has promised me a pearl necklace. I'm all in a lather he might change his mind."

That really jolted me. She was looking directly at me and there was a cold glitter in her eyes, the kind of glitter Janey had sometimes when she was after something from me she thought might be hard to get.

"This won't take me three minutes," I said. "Just relax."

In less than that time I had the safe open.

"Some safe!" she said. "Why, a kid could open it!"

I was looking inside the safe. Stacked on three shelves were packets of hundred dollar bills. I've never seen so much money. I couldn't make a guess how much there was—probably half a million dollars.

The girl slid off the settee and joined me by the safe. I could smell her perfume and her arm touched mine: that was how close we were together.

"Aladdin's Cave!" she said breathlessly. "Oh boy! Wouldn't it be nice to help ourselves!"

I heard the tinkle of the telephone bell, warning me Cooper had finished speaking. It warned the girl too for she hurriedly returned to the settee.

I shut the safe door as Cooper came into the room.

"Haven't you got it open yet?" he barked at me.

"One second, sir," I said and clicked back the lock. "It's open now."

He tried the safe door, opening it only a few inches, then he grunted.

"You'd better get me a duplicate key."

I said I would do that. I packed my tools and started for the door.

I said good-night to the girl on the settee. She just nodded to me. At the front door Cooper gave me a couple of dollars. He gave them grudgingly. He said if ever he needed service in the future for me to give it faster than this time. He told me not to forget the duplicate key.

As I drove back to the depot, I thought about the money in Cooper's safe.

For years now I had been dissatisfied with the money I had been earning. For years I had realised I was never going to get anywhere in this job of mine.

I thought what I could do with that money if it were mine. I thought how easy it would be to break into that apartment, open that sardine can of a safe and help myself.

I told myself I wasn't going to do it, but the thought stayed with me. It was still with me the following night when Roy Tracey came in to relieve me.

I had known Roy most of my life. We had gone to school together, and his father had put him to work with the Lawrence Safes Corporation the same day my father had the same bright idea for me.

In appearance Roy was a lot like me: he was tall and dark and heavily built. He wore a pencil line moustache that gave him an Italian look. He had the same itch for money as I had.

Unlike me, women had no place in his life. He had been married when he was nineteen, but it hadn't worked out. The girl had left him after a year and that finished women for him. His one mania was playing the horses. He was always short of money and was always trying to borrow off me.

I told him about Cooper's money.

We were alone together in the office. It was raining hard, and rain streamed down the windows. I was in no hurry to get home. I told Roy about the girl in Cooper's apartment and how I had opened the safe.

"At a guess there's around half a million in hundred dollar bills," I said, wandering around the office while Roy sat at the desk, smoking. "Imagine owning that kind of money."

"Some guys have all the luck."

"Yeah." I went to the window and stared out into the wet night. "Well, I guess I'll go home. Some night!"

"Don't run away," Roy said. "A half a million? As much as that?"

"It can't be less. There were three shelves of it."

"Sit down. Let's talk about it." We looked at each other. There was a tense expression in his eyes. "I could use money like that, Chet."

I sat down. My heart was beginning to thump.

"So could I."

"I'm in the hole for five hundred bucks," he said. "I've got to get some money. Look, suppose we knock this safe off?" He tilted back his chair, staring at me. "It sounds a soft touch."

"It could be."

There was a pause while we both stared at the rain, beating against the window.

Finally, Roy said, "I've been waiting for a chance like this for some time. I'm fed up living the way I live. You've the same idea, haven't you?"

"Yes."

"Well, how about it? Do you want to do it?"

"No, I don't want to do it, but it's got to be done. It's too easy to pass up."

He grinned at me.

"Don't look so scared. If we use our heads, we'll get away with it."

I sat on the edge of the desk.

"Yes."

"Let's work on it. Let's talk about it."

We spent the next hour making plans. The more we talked about it, the easier it seemed.

"We've got to find out when this guy leaves his apartment. That's the one thing we must know," Roy said. "Once we know that, then we move in, open the safe and help ourselves. Here's what you do. You take the duplicate key he wants to his place and talk to the doorman. He'll tell you when Cooper is out. Doormen like to talk. He'll tell you if you handle him right." He blew smoke at me. "When we know he's out, we walk in and pick up the money."

Put like that it seemed the simplest and easiest job in the world.

II

The next evening I went down to the Ashley Arms. I was wearing the Lawrence Safes Corporation uniform: a buff blouse, bottle green slacks and a peak cap with a badge.

Roy had said he would meet me with the truck as soon as he was off duty. I got to the Ashley Arms a little after ten-thirty.

The doorman was in his office, thumbing through a paperback, a bored expression on his face.

He recognised me as I came into the lobby and nodded to me.

"You again? If you're looking for Mr. Cooper you're unlucky. He's out."

"When will he be back?" I asked, leaning up against the counter and taking out a pack of cigarettes.

The doorman glanced up at the wall clock.

"In half an hour."

"I'll wait. I have a special delivery for him."

"Leave it with me. I'll give it to him."

I shook my head.

"I can't do that. It's the key of his safe. I have to hand it to him personally and get a receipt."

He shrugged his shoulders, taking the cigarette I offered him. "Please yourself."

"Are you sure he'll be back in half an hour?"

"Yeah. He never misses. He leaves here at eight and gets back at eleven."

"Some guys are like that," I said. "You can set a clock by them."

"He's one of them. He owns three night clubs. He checks them every night. Sundays included. He comes back here for dinner at eleven, then he goes out again around one o'clock to see the clubs shut down and count the loot. He never misses."

"Are you on duty all night?" I asked casually.

"I go off at one. After one, we lock up here. Everyone living here has a key." The doorman scowled. "You'd be surprised the number of times I get dragged out of bed because some dope has forgotten his key."

This was falling right into my lap.

"Cooper lost the key to his safe the other night," I said. "He loused up my evening."

"A great guy for losing keys," the doorman said bitterly. "Only last week he lost his door key. He had me out of my bed at five o'clock in the morning for Pete's sweet sake!"

"Is that the time he gets back?"

"Yeah, then sleeps all day . . . the way some guys live!"

I now had the information I wanted. I casually changed the subject. We chewed the fat about this and that until Cooper came in.

He came in a minute to eleven o'clock.

I crossed the hall and met him half way.

"I have the key to your safe, sir," I said.

It took him a moment or so to recognise me.

"Oh, you." He scowled at me. "Let's have it then."

"I'd better see if it's okay, sir. If I could come up . . ."

"Oh, sure."

He led the way to the elevator.

Reaching the third floor, he unlocked his front door and I followed him into the lounge.

I tried the key in the safe door while he stood over me. A wild idea flashed into my mind that when I opened the safe door I'd turn on him, knock him out and help myself to his money, but I didn't do it. Instead, I relocked the safe and handed him the key.

"It's okay, sir."

"Right." He put the key in his pocket. "Thanks." He said it grudgingly and his hand went to his pocket, but that was as far as it went. I could read his mind. He had already given me two bucks. He was telling himself that was plenty.

That little act of meanness decided me. For the past twenty-four hours I had been in two minds about taking his money, but I had only wanted an excuse to push me over the line. He had given it to me.

I left him, took the elevator to the ground floor, waved to the doorman and went out into the rain.

Roy was sitting in the truck, waiting for me.

"Was that Cooper? The fat punk with the red face?"

"That's him." I got into the truck beside Roy. "There's nothing to it," I went on as he drove the truck into the street. "We can skin him on Sunday."

We decided to do the job on Sunday because both of us were off duty then. Roy hired a car and we were set to go.

It was a drowning wet night which was a good thing for us. The rain kept people off the streets, not that there were ever many people wandering around at one o'clock in the morning in this one-horse town.

Roy picked me up at my place and we drove to the Ashley Arms, arriving there, as planned, at five minutes to one a.m.

Roy slid the car between a Cadillac and a Packard in the private parking lot with about forty other cars left out in the rain.

We sat side by side, watching the front entrance of the building. We were both pretty worked up. I could hear Roy's breathing coming fast through his short, thick nose, and I wondered if he could hear my heart pounding.

As the hands of the dashboard clock moved to the hour, we saw Cooper come out and cross over to a white Jaguar, parked ten yards from where we waited. He came out, running, his head bent against the rain, and he didn't look our way. We watched him slide his bulk into the car and then drive off into the darkness.

11

"That's one of them out of the way," Roy said. His voice sounded husky and unsteady.

A few minutes later we saw the doorman close the glass doors of the main entrance and turn the key. We watched him through the glass doors walk across the lobby and disappear down the stairs to the basement.

"Let's go," Roy said and opened the car door.

My heart was pounding so hard I was short of breath. I grabbed up my tool kit and slid out of the car. The rain felt cold against my face as I ran to the glass doors.

We knew exactly what we had to do. I was to open the doors while Roy kept watch.

There was a long drive-in to the block and the entrance couldn't be seen from the street. Unless someone living in the apartment block unexpectedly showed up, we were reasonably safe.

I had trouble with the lock of the glass doors. In an ordinary way, I would have fixed it in three or four seconds, but my hands were shaking. I finally got the doors open as Roy began to curse me.

He joined me as I pushed open the doors and we walked silently and quickly to the stairs. We had decided not to use the elevator in case the doorman hadn't gone to bed and wondered who was around.

We walked up the stairs. We didn't meet anyone. Both of us were panting when we reached Cooper's front door.

This time I had no trouble with the lock. The first key I tried unlocked it.

I pushed open the door and stepped into the dark hall. Roy crowded in after me. For some moments we stood motionless, listening. We heard only a clock ticking somewhere and the occasional rumble of the refrigerator in the kitchen.

"Come on! come on!" Roy said. "What are we waiting for?"

I moved into the lounge and turned on the light.

Roy followed me and shut the door.

"He certainly knows how to live, doesn't he?" he said as he looked around. "Where's the safe?"

I went over to the fat nude and swung aside the frame. I spun the dial, setting the combination. Then using the key I had cut when I had cut Cooper's duplicate key, I unlocked the safe and pulled open the door.

"Take a look!"

Side by side, we stood staring at the neatly stacked piles of hundred dollar bills.

"Gee!" Roy's fingers gripped my arm. "This'll put us on easy street for the rest of our lives!"

Then we both heard a sound that froze us: the unmistakable

sound of a key being pushed into a lock and the lock snapping back.

I was so scared I couldn't move. I just managed to turn my head to stare at the closed door, but the rest of me was paralysed.

But not Roy.

For a split second, he remained frozen, then he became alive. He slid away from me with the quickness of a lizard. He snapped off the light as the door pushed open.

The light from the hall fell into the darkened room, making a rectangle of hard white light in which I stood.

Standing in the doorway was the long legged blonde. For maybe a second we stared at each other.

Then she started back and let out a scream that went through my head like a red hot wire.

"There's someone in here!" she yelled. "It's a burglar!"

Cooper's bulky frame loomed up behind her. He pushed her aside and came storming into the darkened room.

All this happened so fast I was still standing in front of the open safe, scared silly and unable to move.

The girl bolted out of the apartment and started down the stairs, screaming like a train whistle.

I could see Roy's dim outline as he pressed himself against the wall by the door. As Cooper came into the room, he didn't see Roy. He was glaring at me and his hands were extended as if he were going to grab me by the throat. Roy moved silently. I saw him swing the heavy crowbar we had brought with us in case we had trouble with the locks. He slammed it down on Cooper's head as Cooper made a grab at me.

Cooper went down like a felled ox. His clawed fingers scraped down the front of my coat as he fell.

"Quick!" Roy gasped. "Out!"

We could hear the girl screaming as she bolted down the stairs. I rushed to the door.

"Chet!" Roy's voice came behind me in a hiss of fear. "Not down! Up!"

But I was already on the stairs, going down. My mind was frozen with panic. I had only one thought—to get out into the open and to get away.

"Chet!"

I heard him, but I kept on. I reached the second floor and started a blind rush to the head of the stairs. An apartment door facing me opened, and a thin, white haired scared looking man peered out. We glared at each other, then he hurriedly slammed the door shut.

I took the next flight of stairs in three thudding jumps, lost my balance and sprawled on the landing. I struggled to my feet and dived frantically down the last flight of stairs into the lobby.

The long legged blonde was crouching by the doorman's office door. She stared in horror at me, her red lips parted and this nerve jarring scream coming out of her.

The doorman, in shirt and trousers, his hair standing on end, came charging up from the basement and flung himself at me. We went down together in a heaving, thrashing assortment of arms and legs.

I hit him about the head and body and I took a couple of stiff pokes in the face before I threw him off. I staggered up and made a dive for the door.

As I got it open, the doorman began blowing a police whistle. This whistle and the girl's screams made an inferno of sound that galvanised me into the rain.

I ran down the drive into the street. I could still hear the girl's screams, but the piercing blast of the police whistle rose above any noise she could make.

With my heart pounding and sweat running down my face, I bolted down the street. I heard a man's voice yell after me. I looked back to see a shadowy outline of a man in a peak cap, pounding down the street after me.

I kept on running, then I heard the bang of a gun. Something that sounded like a hornet zipped past my face.

I dodged frantically and darted across the street to where it was darker.

The gun banged again. I felt a giant's hand thump on my back and I sprawled face down in the road. White hot pain bit into me. I tried to roll over, but the pain paralysed me.

The last thing I remembered before I blacked out was the sound of pounding feet coming towards me.

CHAPTER TWO

I

I BECAME aware of voices, out of focus, coming from a long way off: voices whispering to me from the end of a mile-long tunnel.

Then I became aware of a hot, dull ache in the middle of my chest, a pain that grew as I slowly climbed out of the dark pit into which I had fallen.

I half opened my eyes.

White walls surrounded me. There was a dim shape of a man bending over me. He didn't come into focus, and as the pain bit into me more sharply, I shut my eyes.

But my mind was now active. I remembered the rush down the three flights of stairs, the fight with the doorman, the wild terrified screams of the long-legged blonde and my blind, stupid rush into the street. I heard again the two bangs from the cop's gun.

Well, I was caught. My futile attempt to grab some easy money had finished in a hospital bed with a cop standing over me.

"If he's not all that badly hurt," a voice said suddenly, "why can't I shake the punk and snap him out of it?"

A tough, hard cop voice you hear on the movies and can never imagine ever talking that way to you.

"He'll come out of it," another voice said. "No point in rushing things, sergeant. He's had a lucky escape. Another inch to the right and he would have been a dead man."

"Yeah? I bet he'll wish he was dead by the time I'm through with him."

I was alert now and I peered at the two men standing by my bed. One of them was soft and fat and in a white overall: he would be the croaker. The other was a big man, fleshy with a red blunt-featured face, small hard eyes and a mouth like a razor cut. His shabby, dark clothes and the way he wore his hat told me who he was: he was a cop, the owner of the tough voice.

I lay still, riding the pain in my chest. I began to wonder what had happened to Roy.

15

He hadn't panicked the way I had. He had gone up the stairs while I had rushed blindly down into the arms of the law. Had he got away?

Unless he had been seen leaving the building, he was in the clear. I was the one who had been caught. I was the one who had seen the money in Cooper's safe. I was the one who had talked to the doorman about Cooper's movements. I was the one who had been seen running down the stairs. Roy was out of all this.

Then I remembered the sound the crowbar had made as Roy had slammed it down on Cooper's head. It had been a terrible blow: made terrible by a viciousness I hadn't expected to be in Roy.

I experienced a sudden feeling of sick fear. What had happened to Cooper? Had Roy killed him?

Then I became aware of the smell of stale sweat and tobacco smoke so close that I opened my eyes and found myself staring up into the cop's red, brutal face.

We were alone. I hadn't heard the doctor leave, but he must have gone, for he wasn't in the room.

The cop grinned at me, showing his tobacco-stained teeth. It was like a wolf grinning at me.

"Okay, punk," he said. "Let's have it. I've been waiting two days and nights to talk to you. Let's have it."

That was the beginning of it.

They seemed to have a vague idea I hadn't done the job alone. They had nothing to go on, but they kept at me, trying to find out if I had had someone with me. I said no, and I kept on saying no.

They told me Cooper was dying and I would be up on a murder charge. If I had had someone working with me, now was the time to spill it. I told them I had handled the job alone.

Finally, they got tired of trying to make me admit I wasn't alone. Finally, too, they had to tell me that Cooper was recovering. They seemed pretty sore that he was going to recover.

"But you could have killed him," the sergeant with the tobacco-stained teeth told me, "and that'll make an impression on the judge. You'll get ten years for this, punk, and you'll regret every one of them."

From the hospital I was transferred to the State Jail. I remained there for three months while they got Cooper into good enough shape to give evidence against me.

I'll remember the trial for as long as I live.

When I was brought into the court room, I looked around. The first person I spotted in the spectators' gallery was Janey. That surprised me. She waved her hand at me and I managed somehow to smile in return. She was the last person I expected to see there.

16

Then there was Franklin, my boss at the Lawrence Safes Corporation, and sitting by his side was Roy.

Roy and I looked at each other for a brief moment. Roy looked pale and thin. I imagined he had been sweating it out during those three months, wondering if I were going to give him away.

The judge was a little guy with a thin, mean face and stony eyes. I didn't stand a chance of beating the rap.

Cooper, much thinner, with his head in bandages, told how I had come to open the safe and how he had asked me for a duplicate key.

The long-legged blonde got onto the witness stand. She had on a sky blue dress that showed off her curves in a way that had every man in the court room, including the judge, staring at her.

She explained that she sang at one of Cooper's clubs and from time to time she visited his apartment to discuss with him the songs she wanted to sing. Everyone in court knew why she visited Cooper's apartment at one o'clock in the morning, and you could see by the way they looked at Cooper how much they envied him. She said Cooper had been out of the room when I had opened the safe. She said she saw me look inside the safe, then shut the door and pretend I hadn't opened it.

Cooper told the judge how he had found me in front of the open safe. He said when he had closed with me, I had hit him on the head with an iron bar.

Franklin surprised me by coming forward and speaking for me. He said I was the best workman they had, and up to now they had always found me completely trustworthy. But he was wasting his breath. I could see he made as much impression on the judge as a handful of grit thrown at an armoured truck.

My attorney, a well-fed, middle-aged chisler, seemed to have trouble in keeping awake. After he had heard the evidence for the prosecution, he looked over at me, grimaced, got slowly to his feet and announced that his client—that was me—now pleaded guilty and threw himself on the mercy of the court. Maybe there wasn't anything else he could do, but I felt at least he might have made it sound as if he were sorry. The way he said it, I and everyone in the court got the impression he was already concentrating on his next case.

The judge stared at me for several sadistic moments. Finally he said I had committed a breach of trust. In my particular job a man had to be trustworthy. I had endangered the reputation of an old-established firm where my grandfather and my father had served as faithful servants. He said that as this was my first offence he had been tempted to treat me leniently. He didn't kid me for one moment. I could tell by his hard little eyes that he was talking for the sake of hearing his own voice. He said my brutal,

2   17

savage attack on Cooper—an attack that might have ended in a murder charge—had placed me beyond the mercy of the court. He then sentenced me to ten years' penal servitude. I would be sent to the Farnworth Prison Camp where they would know how to deal with a man of my viciousness.

That was the moment when I was tempted to betray Roy, and he knew it. I turned to look at him and our eyes met. He was tense and sitting bolt upright. He knew what was going on in my mind. He knew I had only to point to him and tell the judge he was the man who had hit Cooper for me to get off the hook for at least a couple of months for a new trial, and maybe, if it could be proved that Roy had hit Cooper, for me not to go to Farnworth.

Farnworth was a notorious chain gang prison farm, some two hundred miles in the interior, and had been the subject of a number of newspaper articles over the past three years when public spirited journalists had called on the authorities to close the camp, which they described as the nearest thing to a Nazi concentration camp as made no difference.

I had read the articles, and like a lot of people, I had been shocked by what I had read. If the newspaper men were telling the truth, the conditions at Farnworth were as horrible as they were disgraceful.

The thought of serving ten years in that hell-hole made my blood run cold.

Roy and I looked at each other. As we stared at each other, I remembered a lot of small, unimportant things he had done for me when we had been at school together and when we had worked together. I remembered his jeering, friendly sympathy when my girl friends had let me down. I remembered the long talks we had had together and the plans we had made if we ever got hold of some money. It was those things that made it impossible for me to betray him. I gave him a grin: it wasn't much of a grin, but at least it told him he was safe.

I felt a heavy hand of one of the cops who had stood by my side during the trial drop on my arm.

"Get moving," the cop said under his breath.

I looked at Janey, who was sobbing into her handkerchief. I looked at Roy again, then I went down the steps out of sight of the court, out of the world of freedom into a future that held no hope for me. The only thought that kept me going while I waited to be taken to Farnworth was that I hadn't betrayed Roy.

That thought helped me to keep my self-respect: and because of where I was going, that was something I just had to hang onto.

II

Farnworth wasn't a prison of high walls and cells. It was a prison of chains, sharp-shooting guards and savage dogs.

If the days were terrible, the nights were worse. At the end of each day, seventy-seven stinking, unwashed men were herded like cattle into a bunk-house fifty feet long and ten feet wide with one small barred window and an iron-studded door. Each man was shackled to a chain that circled the bunkhouse. He was shackled in such a way that whenever he moved the other men were jerked awake by the communal chain tightening.

After a day in the burning sun, working until every bone in your body ached, the slightest irritation became intolerable. Often when a man was restless in his sleep and jerked the chain, his neighbour struck at him, and vicious fights were continually breaking out in the stifling darkness.

Once we were locked in the bunk-house, the guards left us alone until the morning. They didn't care how many fights broke out, and if anyone got murdered, it meant just one less for them to bother about.

There were only twelve guards to look after the prisoners. At night they went off duty with the exception of one man. This man, Byefleet by name, was in charge of the dogs. There was something so savage and primitive about him that even the dogs were scared of him.

The dogs were kept in a big steel pen during the day and they were kept short of food. They were as dangerous as tigers.

At seven o'clock each night, the prisoners were chained to their bunks and the guards went off duty. It was then Byefleet, a giant of a man, fat, with the face of a pig, came into his kingdom. Carrying a baseball club, he would go to the steel pen and let the dogs out.

No one except this pig of a man dared to move into the open before half-past four in the morning when the dogs were herded back into their pen and the guards came on duty.

Night after night I lay sleepless in my bunk while I listened to the snarling of the dogs as they walked around the buildings that made up the prison farm.

Before I could escape from this hell-hole I knew I would have to find some way of fixing those dogs.

From the moment I stepped inside Farnworth prison I had made up my mind to escape. I had been in this prison now for ten days, and already they were ten days too many. If it hadn't been for the dogs, I would have crashed out after the first night and taken my chance of being shot down. Neither the lock on my ankle chain nor the lock on the bunk-house door presented any difficulties.

During my first terrible night in the bunk-house, I had managed to loosen a piece of wire from the grill that served as my mattress, and after a struggle that left my fingers bleeding, I had succeeded in breaking off a strand some three inches long. With that and a little patience I could fix any Farnworth lock.

It drove me half crazy to know I could escape from this stinking bunk-house if it hadn't been for those snarling dogs out there in the darkness. Somehow I had to dream up an idea to fool them.

During the days that followed, I came to the conclusion that an escape attempt in daylight was out of the question.

Every morning we were marched to the fields, guarded by six guards armed with automatic rifles and on horseback.

The road to the fields was as bare of cover as the back of my hand. Long before I could reach the distant highway or the river, I would have been shot down by one of the guards who would come after me on his horse.

If I were to escape, the attempt would have to be made at night, but first I would have to think of a way to fool those dogs.

So during the day, while I toiled in the fields and most of the night as I lay in my stinking bunk, I wracked my brains as to how I could lick those dogs, but nothing came up that was of any use.

Each morning as we paraded for the roll call, I passed the dog pen. There were ten dogs in the steel cage: massive brutes, some Alsatians, some wolf hounds. A man on his own attempting to escape wouldn't stand a chance against those ten dogs. They would concentrate on him and tear him to pieces before he got twenty yards from the bunk-house.

The problem baffled me.

It wasn't until I had been at Farnworth for close on a month that I solved the problem.

I was put on kitchen fatigue: a job every prisoner dreaded.

The food dished up for the prisoners was practically uneatable. The invariable diet was potato soup in which floated lumps of half rotten meat. Working in the kitchen in the heat and the ghastly stink of rottening meat was an experience to turn the strongest stomach.

To disguise the taste of the meat, the cook used a lot of pepper, and it was this pepper that gave me the idea of fixing the dogs.

For the next three days when I returned to the bunk-house I brought back with me a pocketful of pepper which I hid in a flour sack in my bunk.

I was now two steps forward in my escape plan. I had the means of opening the door of the bunk-house and I had a quantity of pepper to throw the dogs off my scent once I reached the river.

But if the dogs spotted me, no amount of pepper would save me. The pepper would only serve a purpose if I could get out of sight of the dogs, and they then came after me, trying to follow my scent.

But how was I to reach the cover of the river before the dogs spotted me?

If I could solve this problem, I was ready to go.

For the next four days I concentrated on the sounds going on outside the bunk-house. These sounds gave me a picture of Byefleet's routine, and I needed that.

At seven o'clock in the evening, when it was still light, Byefleet took over from the guards. The prisoners were checked and driven into the bunk-house where one of the trusties fastened on the chains while Byefleet watched. Then the bunkhouse was locked up and Byefleet went over to the dog pen and let the dogs out. Then he went to a hut where there was a bed and lay down: maybe he even slept. With ten dogs doing his work there was no reason why he shouldn't sleep.

At a quarter to four in the morning, he left the hut and went over to the kitchen to collect a couple of buckets of meat scraps for the dogs. He carried these buckets into the steel pen and the dogs followed him in. From the noise and the sudden yelps of pain, I guessed he stood over the dogs, supervising them, this took a little time. Then at twenty minutes past four, he locked up the pen and walked over to the steam whistle. He gave it a couple of long, ear-splitting blasts. This was to wake the prisoners and tell the guards the dogs were back their pens.

This routine never varied. I decided my only chance of escape was to crash out as soon as the dogs began to feed.

I would only have a small margin of time to get to the river: a distance of a mile across completely flat ground. I was in good physical shape and I was fast on my feet. I could reach the river in under six minutes, but they could be hectic minutes. Only there I would begin to use my store of pepper to blot out my trail. I would keep going until they came after me, then I would hide somewhere until they got tired of looking for me. From then on I would move only at night. I would head for the railway which was about twenty miles from Farnworth. I then planned to jump a train that would take me to Oakland, the biggest town in the district, where I could get lost.

There was one more thing to worry me. It wouldn't take a second or so to unlock my ankle chain, but it would take me longer to open the bunk-house door. While I was doing this, would one of the trusties raise the alarm?

If one of the trusties started yelling, Byefleet might hear him, then I would be sunk.

Having got so far with what looked like a nearly foolproof escape plan, I decided I wasn't going to leave anything to chance if I could help it.

There is always one man in a prison camp more feared than the rest. At Farnworth this man was Joe Boyd.

He was not more than five foot three in height, but in breadth he was twice the size of a normal man. His brutal face was a mass of scars from past ferocious fights. His smashed nose spread across his face and his tiny, gleaming eyes peered out from under bushy eyebrows. He looked like an orang outang, and acted like one.

He slept in a bunk below mine. If I could persuade him to come with me, I was sure no one in the bunk-house would dare raise the alarm while I worked on the door.

But could I trust him not to give me away?

I knew nothing about him. He never spoke to anyone. He kept to himself, but if anyone came too close to him, his enormous fist would crash into their faces, stunning them.

It would be easy enough to tell him my plan without anyone else overhearing me. All I had to do was to pull aside the filthy blanket covering the wire grill on which I lay, and I would be looking right down on him.

I spent half the night listening to his violent snoring, and wondering about him. He was hated not only by the prisoners but also by the guards. I couldn't imagine him giving me away, and finally around two o'clock in the morning I decided to take a chance and include him in my escape plan.

I undid my ankle chain and pulled aside the blanket.

I couldn't see him down there in the darkness, but I could smell him and I could hear his heavy, snorting breathing.

"Boyd!"

My voice was low-pitched and tense.

His heavy breathing abruptly stopped. He had come awake the way an animal comes awake, and I imagined him staring up into the darkness, his little ape's eyes flickering and suspicious.

"Boyd! Are you listening?"

"Huh?"

The grunt was soft but alert.

"I'm crashing out in a couple of hours," I said, keeping my voice to a whisper. "Are you coming with me?"

"Crashing out?"

"When Byefleet is feeding the dogs, I'm getting out. Are you coming with me?"

"You're nuts! How the hell can you get out?"

"I've got the ankle chain off already and I can get yours off. I can open the door. Are you coming with me?"

"How about the dogs?"

"I told you: when Byefleet is feeding them, we'll go."

"Go—where?"

"To the river. With any luck we'll get to the railway. It's worth a try. If you don't want to come, say so."

"You can get this goddamn chain off?"

"Yes."

"Then get it off!"

I slid off the bunk and down on the floor beside him. I felt along his massive leg until my groping hands reached the ankle chain. Working in the dark made my task tricky, but after a few minutes I turned the lock and the anklet dropped onto the blanket.

As I straightened, two hot, sweating hands groped for me out of the darkness, slid up my shirt front and before I could get out of his reach, his fingers fastened around my throat.

He had a grip like a vice. He nipped my breath off. I didn't attempt to struggle. I remained on my knees beside him, praying he wasn't going to murder me.

Suddenly he let go and his hand caught my shirt front, pulling me against him.

"Listen, punk," he snarled, "if you're figgering to get me in a jam . . ."

For a moment I struggled to get my breath back into my lungs, then I managed to hiss at him: "Go to hell, you ape! If you don't want to come, say so!"

Someone close to us moaned in his sleep. Someone cursed softly. We were whispering together. I could smell his rotten breath. This seemed to be the way to talk to him. His hand slid off my shirt.

"Yeah, I'll come."

"As soon as we get out, we run for the river," I said. "When we reach the river we split up. They'll send the dogs after us. If we can reach the river we can fool the dogs. Can you swim?"

"Never mind what I can do," he snarled. "You open that door. I'll take care of myself."

I climbed back onto my bunk and lay there, fingering my throat. The first faint light of dawn was beginning to show at the window. In an hour it would be time to make a start.

I got out the sack of pepper and put it inside my shirt. I wasn't going to share the pepper with Boyd. I might need every grain of it before I got clear of the dogs.

23

I lay there waiting, watching the light become stronger and listening to Boyd's heavy breathing.

I heard him whisper suddenly, "You sure you can open the door?"

I rolled over so I could speak to him.

"I'm sure."

"What makes you think we'll get away with this?"

"Anything's better than staying here."

"Yeah."

There was a long silence. Then we heard two of the dogs snarling at each other. The sound chilled my blood.

"Those dogs . . ." Boyd muttered.

"Once they start eating they won't bother us," I said.

"That's what you hope," Boyd said, and I caught the fear in his voice.

Even a brutal ape like Boyd was scared of those dogs.

Forty long tense minutes crawled by. A thin dagger of sunlight began to move across the floor of the bunk-house, telling me I had now only a few more minutes before the crash out.

My heart was thumping and my hands sweating. I could hear the dogs snarling outside. A number of the prisoners began to stir, jerking each other awake with the communal chain and beginning to curse each other.

I could see Boyd's face now as I looked down at him.

"You're going ahead with this?" he said. "You're not kidding?"

"I'm not kidding," I said.

The snarling of the dogs suddenly turned to excited barks. That told me Byefleet was making his way from the hut to the kitchen.

"Watch it one of these guys don't start yelling while I'm working on the door," I said to Boyd.

"I'll watch it," Boyd said, and sitting up, he swung his massive legs to the floor.

I slid off the bunk and crossed to the door.

One of the trusties, a rat-faced, bald-headed little man, jerked upright on his bunk.

"Hey, you! Whatja tink ya doin'?" he bawled.

Boyd came to his feet. He waddled over to the trustie and slammed his fist in his face. The trustie dropped back, blood pouring from his crushed nose.

Boyd stood in the middle of the bunk-house, his hands on his enormous hips and glared around.

"Anyone else want to start something?" he snarled.

No one moved. By now they were all sitting up staring goggled-eyed at me.

24

The lock proved easier than I expected. I got the door open as I heard Byefleet's bellowing voice cursing the dogs.

"Let's go!" I said, aware my voice had shot up a note and feeling cold sweat running down my spine.

I moved cautiously out into the cool morning air.

To my right, not more than fifty yards from me, was the dog pen. I saw Byefleet, his back turned to me, pouring a bucket of meat and mash into a trough. The dogs were snarling and snapping at each other as they pressed forward to get at the food.

Boyd joined me. He, too, looked across at the dog pen.

"Come on!" I said and started to run.

I felt naked and scared as I started across that flat stretch of ground with the river so far in the distance.

I could hear Boyd thudding after me. I could also hear him panting. He wasn't in my class as a runner, and I quickly shot ahead.

I've never run so fast in my life. I flung myself over the ground, seeing the long line of reeds that guarded the river coming more sharply into focus.

Then I heard the bang of a gun.

I slowed a little and looked back over my shoulder.

Byefleet was out of the dog pen, crouching, holding a .45. He fired again, and I saw a spurt of dust five feet or so to the left of Boyd, who was running doggedly but not making much speed. It was pretty rotten shooting.

I could hear the snarling and snapping of the dogs. They were too busy to come after us and that gave me heart. I quickened my pace again, and when I was within a hundred yards of the reeds I again looked back.

Boyd was nearly two hundred yards behind me, but he kept coming.

The steam whistle was now blasting, and I knew within a very few minutes the guards would be after us.

I crashed through the reeds, belted along the bank of the river. After I had gone a hundred yards I threw myself down behind a thick shrub.

Some seconds later I heard Boyd blunder into the reeds. He wasn't more than twenty yards from me, but the reeds were too thick for him to see me.

"Hey! Damn you! Where are you?" he panted, pausing to look left and right.

I kept still. I didn't want him with me. I wanted to split the hunt.

He waded into the river, paused to look back, then began to swim strongly towards the opposite bank.

I took out the sack of pepper and filled the turn-ups of my

trousers with the stuff. Then I began to move fast and silently along a path between the high bank and the reeds. And when I was sure Boyd, as he swam, couldn't hear me, I began to run again.

I had gone some distance along the bank when I heard the horses. Now was the time to hide, and I looked around for a likely place. I found it in a thicket a few yards from the bank. I crawled under cover and lay flat, sweat streaming off me and my heart pounding.

The sound the horses made as they crashed about among the reeds was alarmingly close.

There was a sudden shout and then the sound of the splashing of water. I guessed one of the guards was swimming his horse across the river.

Then I heard a voice bawl, "I can see him!" There was the sound of a rifle shot.

Another horse splashed into the river. There was more shooting.

I edged forward, pushing aside the undergrowth so I could see. A guard, swimming his horse across the river, holding an automatic rifle in his hand, came into sight.

As he urged his horse up the opposite bank, there was more shooting, closer. Then I saw Boyd suddenly break cover and dive into the river. He began to swim frantically towards where I was hiding. I watched him come.

The guard who had just got out of the river slid off his horse, and kneeling on the bank, he lifted his rifle.

Boyd must have sensed his danger. He dived as the guard fired. The bullet kicked up a spurt of water where Boyd's head had been.

The other guard, crashing his horse through the undergrowth, appeared on the bank.

"He's swimming back!" the first guard shouted. "Get after him! I'll watch him from here!"

The mounted guard urged his horse once more into the river. As the horse began to swim, Boyd's head bobbed up for a brief moment. He was nearly halfway across the river by now, but the mounted guard had seen him. He swung his horse towards the swimming man just as Boyd dived again. I could see it was going to be an unequal race.

Boyd couldn't reach shelter before the guard caught up with him. He must have realised this himself. He certainly was an expert under-water swimmer. He must have turned under-water and swum towards the guard, for his head bobbed up just behind the swimming horse. The guard didn't see him, but the other guard did and he yelled a warning. Boyd was too close to the mounted guard for the other to risk a shot.

The mounted guard twisted around in his saddle, his face alarmed. He aimed a blow at Boyd's head with the butt of his rifle, but missed him.

With the quickness of a striking snake, Boyd grabbed the guard's wrist and heaved him off his horse into the water.

The guard was helpless in the grip of those brutal hands. The two men disappeared from sight. There was a violent churning of water, and then Boyd bobbed up alone.

He came up with the horse between him and the guard on the bank, and he kept it that way. Holding the horse's bridle, he urged the animal downstream.

The other guard hesitated, then seeing what was happening, and that Boyd now had a chance of escaping, he ran back to his horse, mounted it and forced the animal into the river. He went after Boyd, who was having trouble controlling the swimming horse. He passed close to where I was hiding. His ape-like face was set and white, and I could hear him cursing the horse, trying to urge it forward faster.

The other guard was rapidly overtaking him, but he still couldn't get a shot at him.

I saw Boyd suddenly let go of his horse and dive. I guessed he was going to try to surprise the guard as he had the other, but this time he overplayed his hand.

The guard was alert, and Boyd slightly misjudged his distance. He bobbed up right by the guard. As he frantically shook the water out of his eyes, his hands grabbing at the guard, the guard smashed his rifle butt down on Boyd's head.

Boyd went down like a stone, and where he had sunk the river water turned red.

The guard was taking no chances. He swung his horse around and made for the bank, coming out of the river not far from where I lay.

I recognised him now. His name was Geary. He was a brute and a sadist, and had made my days at Farnworth a hell. If I had had a gun I wouldn't have hesitated to shoot him, but I had no gun so I lay watching him while he sat on his horse, waiting for Boyd's body to come to the surface.

It came up eventually, floating face down and drifted to the bank where I rested among the reeds.

The other horse struggled up onto the bank. Geary moved up to it and took its bridle.

Geary then looked over the surface of the river. He was looking for the other guard's body. I spotted the body on the far side of the bank just a few seconds before he did.

He grunted, then leading the other horse, he went crashing off through the reeds and back to Farnworth.

I waited until the sounds died away, then cautiously I came out of hiding.

They would recover the two bodies, then Byefleet and some of the mounted guards would come after me with the dogs. In the meantime every State trooper would be alerted. The police of the district would be on the look-out for me. A warning would be broadcast.

I had still a long way to go before I was safe—if I ever was going to be safe.

Carrying the sack of pepper, I started off again. The morning sun was up by now, and already there was heat.

As I ran, the pepper kept jerking out of my trousers turn-ups, blotting out my scent.

After about a couple of miles, I pulled up, panting. Now was the time to cross the river. The railway lay on the far side about sixteen miles from where I was.

I took off my trousers and folded them into a small pack in which I put the sack of pepper. I tied the pack on top of my head with my belt, then I walked into the river and swam over to the opposite bank.

CHAPTER THREE

I

THE time was ten minutes after four o'clock in the afternoon. I lay under the shade of a tree on a sloping hill that went away down to the highway.

By keeping to the woods and following the river I had covered quite a distance. No sound of any pursuit had followed me. The pepper idea had paid off. The dogs hadn't been able to pick up my scent.

But I was still five miles from the railway, and now the country had become flat and open. I didn't dare move out of the woods until dark.

Below me on the far side of the highway was a small farm. It wasn't much of a place, consisting of the farmhouse, three big sheds, a barn and a lot of junk lying around. I didn't pay much attention to it until I saw a girl come out of the farmhouse and walk over to one of the sheds. She was carrying two big baskets of cantaloups.

From this distance I couldn't see what she looked like, and I didn't care. My eyes watched those cantaloups and my mouth watered at the sight of them.

When it was dark I would sneak down there and grab myself a few.

There was a heap of traffic on the highway, mostly trucks carrying cantaloups to Oakland. Every now and then a glittering Cadillac or an Oldsmobile would blast its impatient way past the trucks. From time to time I spotted a State trooper on his motorcycle, patrolling, and once, a police radio car.

The hours dragged by.

At six o'clock a battered truck came up the dirt road leading to the farm. It was loaded with cantaloups. I watched it pull up outside one of the sheds.

The girl came out of the farmhouse.

Two men got down off the truck. One of them was young, the other middle-aged.

They all moved over to the farmhouse and I imagined them

29

sitting down to supper, and the thought tormented me. I was hungry enough to think longingly of Farnworth's filthy food.

Another couple of hours crawled by. The sun went down and the stars came out. The traffic had practically ceased. I hadn't seen a State trooper for some time. I decided it would be safe to move.

I reached the highway without seeing a car. There was a light showing in one of the windows of the farmhouse. I had watched for a dog, but hadn't seen one. I crossed the highway at a run and reached the dirt road leading up to the farm.

The farm gate was closed. I climbed it, and then moved away from the farmhouse to one of the sheds.

I paused outside the open door. It was dark in there, but I could smell the cantaloups.

I went in. I had no knife, but I split the cantaloups in my hands. The warm sweet juice and the pulpy flesh quenched my thirst and satisfied my hunger.

I was so tired I could scarcely keep my eyes open. I decided to take a short rest before walking the last five miles to the railway.

I groped my way behind a pile of cantaloups and stretched out on the ground. I could hear the radio coming from the farmhouse, playing dance music. I closed my eyes. This was a lot better than sleeping in that stinking bunk-house at Farnworth. I wondered if I would be able to board a train . . . so far my luck had held . . . so far . . .

I woke with a start that set my heart thumping.

Through the open door of the shed I could see the outline of the distant hills. The sun was coming up in a blood red sky and its pale light filtered into the shed.

As I struggled to my feet, panic gripping me, I realised I had slept like a dead man for more than eight hours.

Already I could hear the rumble of trucks on the highway. I wouldn't dare cross the fields now to the railway.

In my black and grey striped prison uniform I would be spotted by any of the passing truck drivers.

Then I heard sounds from the farmhouse: voices and movements. A little later I smelt ham grilling.

I watched and waited for half an hour or so, then the two men came out, followed by the girl. She was around seventeen and very sun-burned. She wasn't pretty, but she had a good figure, and when she smiled she was attractive.

The three talked together for some moments, then the two men climbed up onto the truck and drove away. The girl went back into the farmhouse.

I made another meal of cantaloups, then I settled down behind a pile of crates.

I was trapped in this shed now until nightfall. Thinking about it, I saw that it might not be such a bad thing. Staying here in comparative safety would give the hunt for me time to cool off.

I rested my head on a rolled up sack and closed my eyes. It was hot in the shed and I dozed off.

I came abruptly awake an hour or so later.

Someone was in the shed.

I could hear movements. Very cautiously I edged to the front of the crates and took a quick look.

The girl was sorting cantaloups into sizes, making three piles of them. She worked quickly and expertly, her back turned to me, her long hair falling over her shoulders as she stooped over the pile.

I watched her, wondering if I dare let her know I was there, and then suddenly realising that she did know I was watching her. She had paused abruptly in her work, then she had gone on again, but without the rhythm she had used before. I knew she was now frightened. I could tell that by the way she fumbled with the cantaloups.

I was sure if I didn't do something fast, she would bolt out of the shed and probably start screaming. I could feel the growing tension in her.

I said very quietly, "Don't be frightened," and I stood up so she could see me.

She whirled around. I was sorry for her. She went white under her tan and she tried to scream, but no sound came.

I must have looked pretty terrible. I hadn't shaved for two days. I was filthy dirty. I was big and tough looking, and I saw I had struck terror into her; that made me feel bad.

"I'm not going to hurt you," I said, watching her as she slowly backed away from me until she reached the wall of the shed. She was wearing a pair of jeans and a red and white cowboy shirt. As she pressed herself against the wall, I could see her small breasts lifting and falling under her shirt.

She said in a tiny, tight voice, "Don't come near me!"

"I'm sorry I frightened you. You frightened me," I said. "I'm the man they're hunting for—from Farnworth. Will you help me?" I kept talking. I was scared she would run out and start screaming. "I'm hungry and I want clothes. Will you give me a break?"

I could see she was getting over the shock and she was relaxing.

"What are you doing here?" she asked.

"I was hungry. I came after the cantaloups last night. Then I was fool enough to fall asleep. I planned to reach the railway while it was dark."

"But they are watching the railway," she said breathlessly and

31

I knew then she was on my side. "It was on the radio last night. That's where they expect you to go."

"Then I guess I'll have to think of something else. I don't want to get you in trouble, but will you help me? If you don't, I'm sunk."

She stared at me for a long moment.

"I've read about Farnworth," she said and moved away from the wall. "Yes, I'll help you. I couldn't have it on my conscience to send any man back there. Are you hungry?"

"That ham smelt pretty good."

She managed a ghost of a smile.

"Wait here."

She went to the door. I watched her. I couldn't be sure if I could trust her but there was nothing else I could do. If she called the cops then it was my bad luck.

When she had gone, I prowled around the shed. She seemed to be gone a long time, then just as I was about to go to the house to see what she was doing, she came back, carrying a bucket of hot water, a towel, soap, a razor and a bundle of clothes.

"I'll get you some food now."

Ten minutes later she was back, carrying a tray. She had cooked me six eggs and four cuts of ham, and she had made me a pot of coffee.

In that time I had shaved and washed and had got into the suit which I guessed was her brother's. It was a little tight, and it was shabby, but I didn't care. It was wonderful to be rid of that filthy prison uniform.

I saw she was watching me curiously as I began to wolf down the food. She sat on a box near me.

"How did you escape?" she asked. "I thought no one could get away from Farnworth."

I told her the whole story. I told her how I had the money itch, how Roy and I had planned the robbery, how I had covered up for Roy. I told her about Farnworth and the dogs, and how I had got away.

She listened, her eyes wide open. It did me good to tell her. It was the first time I had talked to anyone about it.

"If I'm caught," I said, "they'll half kill me. They'll put me in a cell they keep for punishment. Three of the guards will come in with belts. They'll lam into me until they can't lam into me any more. Every day for a week, they'll do that. I've seen men come out of the punishment cell. One of them had lost an eye: another had a broken arm."

She drew in a sharp breath of horror.

"But I'm not going to be caught," I said. "I'd rather die than go back to Farnworth."

COME EASY — GO EASY

By then I had finished the meal and was smoking a cigarette from the pack she had put on the tray. I felt pretty good.

"You mustn't go to the railway," she said. "I can help you get to Oakland if that's where you want to go."

"That's where I want to go. It'll be a jumping off place. How can you do it?"

"In an hour, a truck calls here to pick up these cantaloups," she told me. "The trucker is a boy named Williams. He comes every day. He has a meal here. While he is eating, you can hide in the back of the truck. He goes to Oakland market. He leaves the truck in the market square while he collects the money. You could slip out then and you'd be in Oakland."

That's how I got to Oakland. It turned out to be the easiest thing in the world.

Before the trucker arrived, the girl gave me five dollars, all the money she had. She gave me two packs of cigarettes. She warned me I would only have a few hours start. When her brother returned and missed his clothes she would have to tell him she had given the clothes to me. I would have to get out of Oakland fast, but at least I had nothing to worry about until seven or eight that evening when her father and brother got back.

I tried to thank her, but she didn't want my thanks. She said she couldn't send any man back to Farnworth and, anyway, she thought I had had a lot of bad luck.

As the truck jolted off down the dirt road, I peered out between the crates of cantaloups. She stood looking after the truck in her red and white cowboy shirt and her blue jeans. As the truck turned onto the highway, she raised her hand and waved.

She made a picture I keep in mind; a picture that will stay with me for the rest of my days.

II

On the fifth day of my escape from Farnworth, I reached Little Creek, approximately a thousand miles from Oakland.

Those thousand miles I had put between myself and Oakland had been pretty rugged going. I had been lucky to jump a freight train just outside Oakland, but after twenty hours, travelling through the desert without food or water I began to wonder if I would get off that train alive.

Finally, the train pulled in at Little Creek, and I left the truck without anyone spotting me.

The time was late in the afternoon and the heat was intense. There seemed no one around: the main street was deserted.

I still had a dollar fifty left from the money the girl had given me. I went into a snack bar and ordered a hamburger, a coffee and a quart of ice water.

I looked pretty rough after travelling all that time in the truck. I hadn't shaved, and I was filthy dirty and the suit the girl had given me had taken a beating off the floor of the truck, but it didn't seem to matter how I looked in this town. It was dirty and beaten up itself: one of those dead-end dumps, fast dying on its feet.

While I was eating, I considered what my next move was to be. If I could get over the mountain and down into Tropica Springs I felt I would be far enough away from Farnworth to be safe.

Tropica Springs was about two hundred miles from this desert town. My only chance of getting there was to get a ride from some truck or private car. I reckoned it would have to be a truck. No owner of a private car would give me a ride looking the way I looked now.

The man behind the snack counter had a cheerful, friendly face. I asked him what chance I had of getting a ride in a truck going over the mountain.

He shook his head doubtfully.

"There are trucks passing through here by the dozen," he said, "but I've never seen any of them stop. Maybe you'll be lucky, but it's a long shot." He drew a cup of coffee for himself and leaned on the counter. "Your best bet would be to get to Point of No Return. All trucks stop there to fill up before going over the mountain. You could talk to some of the fellas. Maybe you could persuade one of them to take you."

"Point of No Return? Where's that and what is it?"

"Carl Jenson's place. He's lived there all his life. His father owned it before he did: a filling station and a snack bar. There's no other filling station after Point of No Return for the next hundred and sixty miles, and that's on the other side of the mountain."

"How far is it from here?"

"Fifty miles."

"How do I get there—walk?"

He grinned at me.

"Nothing as painful as that. You're in luck. Mr. Jenson will be in here in a while. He comes into town every three months to buy scrap metal: plenty of that going in this bum town. You talk to him. He's a nice fellow. He'll give you a ride out to his place if you tell him you want to get over the mountain. He's always a good one for helping people out of a hole."

"When will he be in then?"

He glanced over his shoulder at the fly-blown clock.

"About twenty minutes. You stick around. I'll tip you when he comes in. How about another coffee?"

I would have liked one, but my money was running low.

"No, thanks. If you don't mind me hanging around . . ."

He drew a cup of coffee and shoved it at me.

"It's on the house. You look as if you've come a long way."

"Yeah." I rubbed my bristly chin. "I'm joining a pal in Tropica Springs. I've been travelling rough. My pal and I are going into business together. I've been travelling on my thumb to save my money."

"Money . . ." The counter man shook his head glumly. "I've never had enough of it. I wouldn't be in this lousy town now if I had enough to take my wife and kids somewhere where I could earn a fair wage. Can't get far without money." He looked out through the open window to watch a big cream and black Cadillac float past, throwing clouds of dust either side, some of it coming through the window. "Those guys. They never stop here. They're loaded with dough, but they never spend it here. At least Mr. Jenson does all right. They have to stop at his place whether they like it or not. I reckon he has a gold mine out there."

While he was speaking, a big man came in through the open doorway and walked to the bar.

"Let's have a fast coffee, Mike," he said. "I want to get away early today."

He glanced at me and then away. As the counter man drew the coffee, he went on, "How's the wife? I haven't seen her around this trip."

"She's in Wentworth this afternoon, Mr. Jenson," the counter man said. He looked at me. "She'll be sorry to have missed you."

Now I knew he was my man, I looked at him more closely. He stood fully six foot four in his socks and was as broad as two ordinary men. His face was fleshy and sunburned. It was a good face: open, kind and humorous. At a guess he was around fifty-two or three. Although he was big, there wasn't much fat on him. He looked durable: a lot more durable than most men of his age.

The counter man said, "Excuse me, Mr. Jenson, this fella is looking for a ride over the mountain. I told him Point of No Return is the best spot to pick up a truck."

Jenson turned and looked me over, then he smiled.

"How do," he said. "Yeah, Mike's right. You won't get any truckers stopping on the road, but they do stop at my place. Glad to be of help. I'll give you a lift to my place, but you'll have to take your chance with the truckers. Most of them aren't permitted to carry passengers over the mountain: something to do with the insurance."

"Thanks," I said, "if you're sure it won't put you out."

He laughed.

"I'm glad to have company on the drive back. It's a damned awful road. My name's Carl Jenson." He held out a big fleshy hand.

I shook hands with him.

"I'm Jack Patmore," I said, thinking up the name on the spur of the moment.

"Are you heading for Tropica Springs?"

"That's right."

He finished his coffee and dropped a coin on the counter.

"Well, if you're ready . . ."

He shook hands with the counter man as I slid off the stool.

"So long, Mike: be seeing you."

I also shook hands with the counter man, nodding my thanks, then I followed Jenson's enormous bulk out into the burning sunshine.

He led the way to where a ten ton truck stood in the shade. The truck was loaded with scrap metal: rusty iron bedsteads were piled together with rods, bolts and broken farm equipment.

Jenson swung himself up into the cab and I followed him. It was like an oven in the cab and we both stripped off our coats.

Jenson took out a pack of cigarettes and offered me one. As we lit up, he said, "May as well make ourselves comfortable. It's a long, hot run." Then he started the engine and drove down the dusty main street.

Neither of us said anything until we were clear of the town, then Jenson broke the silence by asking casually: "Is this your first visit out here?"

"Yes," I said.

"Me—I was born and raised here. It's a lonely spot and it's goddamn hot, but I like it. You come far?"

"Oakland."

"That's quite a step. Never been there myself. What's it like?"

"Okay."

He glanced at me.

"I wouldn't have guessed you were country bred. What line are you in if it isn't being nosey?"

"I'm in the lock trade. My dad was a locksmith too: runs in the family."

"Locks, eh? Would you know anything about metal?"

"Sure. When I'm not fixing locks I'm building safes, and you've got to know about metal with safes."

"Yeah, that's right."

He rubbed the back of his neck, frowning. We were driving along a dusty road that led through the desert. In the far distance was the mountain. The wheels of the truck churned up the dust that came in through the open cab window, smothering us.

"You wouldn't know anything about car engines, would you?" he asked after a long silence.

"As much as most," I said, wondering what he was getting at. "I can take an engine down if that's what you mean. I once made a new cylinder head for my old man's Ford. That was quite a job, but I did it."

He glanced at me again, and I was aware the sharp blue eyes were going over me intently.

"If you can do that, you know cars," he said. "Are you planning to stay in Tropica Springs?"

I was getting bothered by this steady stream of questions.

"Yes," I said, and looked away from him out of the cab window.

In the distance I could see a hawk hovering, sharp etched against the sky that seemed bleached white with the heat.

"Have you a job waiting for you?" he asked. "What I'm driving at is this: if you're looking for a job, I could give you one."

"You could? What kind of a job?"

"I need a guy who can handle metal and cars. These past two years have been tough going for Lola—that's my wife—and for me. I keep promising myself I'd get help. You seem the kind of young fellow I could get along with. Mind you, the place is pretty lonely and you'd have to do your turn at night shift. The nearest town is Wentworth—twenty miles of desert road, but you'd find the food okay. Lola certainly knows how to cook. She's Italian. You like Italian food?"

"I guess so."

"You wait until you try her spaghetti: never tasted anything so good. You'd have a cabin to yourself. There's a radio. I have a spare T.V. set: you could have that too." He looked hopefully at me. "I'd pay forty bucks and all found. There's nothing to spend your money on. You could get together some capital."

I didn't hesitate for more than a second or so. This was my chance to get lost. Anyway, I could work for him for a few months, get together some money and then move on.

"Sounds fine," I said. "Okay, I'd like to give it a trial."

He grinned at me.

"Then you've got yourself a job, son," he said and reaching out his enormous hand, he patted me on the knee.

CHAPTER FOUR

I

THE first sight I had of Point of No Return was when the truck had panted up a sharp hill and then began to coast down into the valley that was as flat as a plate with ribbed white sand, blinding in the sunshine and dotted with burnt up scrub.

"That's it," Jenson said, pointing, "that's my place."

There was a small bungalow, a couple of low sheds, a bigger and higher shed, three gas pumps, and on the other side of the highway, a cabin. All the buildings were painted sky blue, and they stood out against the whiteness of the sand with startling intensity.

"That cabin on the far side is for you," Jenson said. "That was where I was born. My old man built it with his own hands. I built the bungalow when he passed on. It takes guts to live out here. It's lonely and tough going. I'm lucky to have found a woman who'll share it with me. Without her, I'd be sunk. We're on call every night of the week. You'd be surprised the number of times we have to turn out in the middle of the night. Truckers drive over the mountain at night—it's cooler, and they always stop here for gas. That's why I reckon you'll be a big help to me. With three of us taking turns, the night shift won't be so bad."

We were down in the valley by now. The heat came at us with an edge to it that brought me out in a sticky sweat.

"You feel it?" He seemed proud of the heat. "But at night it's okay. At night, it can be really cool."

He put his great hand on the horn button and gave two long blasts. He looked at me, grinning.

"That's to let Lola know I'm coming. She'll be surprised when she sees you. She's always telling me we don't need a hired hand. The fact is, Jack, it's because I've listened to her for so long, I've never had a fella to help out. You know these Italians—goddamn thrifty. That's the way they're made. Me—I guess I'm pretty careful with my money too, but my wife—land's sake!—she's more than careful. 'What do we want a man here for?' she says. 'If I don't mind getting up at night, why should you?' That's the way she talks." He shook his head. "At my age, it's not right.

38

For more years than I care to remember, I've slaved seventeen hours a day. Okay, I've made money, but I've never had any fun out of it. What do you make money for, Jack? You tell me. What do you make it for?"

"Why, I guess, first for security, then when you have that, you go after some fun," I said, humouring him.

"That's right!" He punched me on the knee. "Security first. Well, I've got that taken care of. Now at fifty-five, I'm going to have some fun. With you here, Lola and me can go into Wentworth every now and then. With you to help out, it's going to be a lot easier here."

But there was a slight doubt in his voice that made me look at him, puzzled. He didn't sound like a man who is sold on what he is saying.

The truck was now pounding along the flat, burning road and we passed a big sign that read:

POINT OF NO RETURN
YOU HAVE BEEN WARNED!
LAST CHANCE FOR GAS FOR 165 MILES
SNACK BAR. REPAIRS. GREASING. SERVICE.

I looked beyond the sign to the three gas pumps and the garage that loomed up towards me.

The service station was bright and gay. There were paths to the bungalow and to the cabin across the highway edged with stones, painted white. There were flowers planted around the gas pumps that made a gay splash of colour. Behind the pumps was a long, low building that housed the snack bar. Beyond the snack bar was the bungalow with bright blue curtains at the windows and a cream coloured front door.

"This is quite a place," I said.

He beamed at me.

"Glad to hear you say it. I've certainly worked at it. You and me—we could do a lot more to it. I've plenty of ideas. Up to now I've had to do it all on my own."

He opened the cab door and climbed down onto the white, burning sand. I followed him down.

If I had owned this place and had a wife to share it with me, and if I had blasted my horn the way Jenson had, I would have expected my wife to have come out from where she was and give me a welcome.

But no one came out of any of the buildings to welcome Carl Jenson back to his home.

The place could have been a morgue for all the excitement his arrival caused, and that registered with me, although it didn't seem to surprise him.

He waved to the cabin.

"You go ahead. You want a wash and a shave." He gave me a nudge in the ribs that made me stagger. "You hungry? I'll get you something. You go ahead and clean up."

"When I'm through—where do I come?"

He pointed to the lunch room.

"Right there," and nodding, he walked up the path to the bungalow.

I went over to the cabin, pushed open the door and walked into the living-room. It was comfortably furnished, and there was a T.V. set in one of the corners. Beyond the living-room was a tiny bedroom. I stripped off my clothes and went into the bathroom. It took me a little time to get clean and shave. By now I had raised quite a moustache, and I decided to keep it. I returned to the bedroom, put on my shirt and trousers, and then took a look at myself in the mirror on the wall.

The moustache made quite a difference, but I was still acutely aware that I was being hunted. Looking at myself now, I felt more secure. If there were pictures of me in the papers, I was pretty sure with this moustache, I wouldn't be recognised.

I went to the cabin door and stood looking across at the opposite buildings, then I looked back at the long winding road disappearing into the hills. The desert stretched either side of me: bleak, hot and desolate. It gave me a feeling of security. The police would be looking for me in Oakland or one of the other big towns. I was pretty sure they wouldn't think to look for me here.

I moved out into the sunshine and crossed over to the lunch room. There were ten fixed stools in front of the counter and five tables along the wall for those who wanted to eat in style. Along the counter were beer and soda spouts. There was a glass case full of pies, baked to a turn, with individual labels on each, reading: *cherry, apple, pineapple, cranberry.* There was a unit containing paper napkins, condiments, ketchup, glasses and knives and forks. Everything was spotlessly clean. On the wall was the menu written in bold, neat printing:

TODAY'S SPECIALS
Fried Chicken
Veal Steaks
Beef Hash
Fruit Pies

Through the half open door behind the counter came the smell of onions frying that made my mouth water. I was just about to tap on the counter to attract attention when I heard Jenson say, "Now look, Lola, you mustn't get worked up like this. I know what I'm doing. This young fella can take care of the place, and we two can go to Wentworth a couple times a week. I don't like you going there alone. It's not right for a woman to go to the movies on her own in a town like Wentworth."

"And why isn't it right?"

She spoke with a strong Italian accent and her voice was shrill. "It isn't right. You're a respectable, married woman. There are guys in Wentworth . . ."

"Are you telling me I go around with men in Wentworth? Is that it?"

"Of course I'm not! I'm just saying it isn't right. With this fella here, you and me can go together. That's what we want, isn't it?"

"I know one thing—I don't want any strangers here! I've told you that a thousand times!"

"I know you've told me, but you're wrong. We've got to have help. How many times did you get up last night? Six—maybe seven times. You need your sleep. With this guy to help us out, we'll get our sleep and we'll get some freedom. When he's on night shift, you and me can go to a movie. You'd like that, wouldn't you?"

"How many more times do I have to tell you?" Her voice was angry and excited. "I don't want strangers here. Besides, he isn't working for nothing, is he? Since when have you started to throw your money about?"

The hard shrill note in her voice bothered me. She sounded vindictive, and in a hell of a rage.

"Stop yelling at me! Let's give him a trial. If you don't like him, well okay, then we'll get rid of him. You'll be glad to have him around. Now let's stop this. How about something to eat?"

"How do you know you can trust him? Do you mean you intend to leave him here to take the money, to have the run of this place while we're in Wentworth? You're crazy!"

I felt it was time to let them know I was here. I went on tiptoe to the door, opened it and let it slam shut. Then I walked heavy footed to the counter.

"Anyone here?" I called.

The angry voices abruptly came silent. There was a pause, then Jenson came out of the kitchen. His fat, good natured face was red, and there was an embarrassed look in his eyes.

"There you are," he said. He looked me over and his expression altered a little. I could see he was relieved and pleased that I now looked presentable. "That's a good cabin, eh? Have you found everything you want?"

"It's fine," I said. The smell of the frying onions was driving me half crazy. "And this too. You've certainly got a place here, Mr. Jenson."

He nodded, but the beaming pride wasn't there. I could see he was still bothered about the argument he had been having with his wife.

"Yeah, it's pretty good." He rubbed his jaw, his eyes shifting away from me. "I guess you must be hungry. I'll see what I can rustle up for you."

"Don't worry about me, Mr. Jenson. You tell me what I'm to have and I'll fix it."

"You stick around. I'll talk to my wife."

He was so embarrassed I felt sorry for him. He was starting back to the kitchen when a dusty Packard pulled up by the gas pumps and the driver honked on his horn.

"Shall I take care of him?" I said.

"It's okay. I'll do it. Time enough for you to start work when you've had something to eat."

He went out and I watched him through the open window as he began to service the car.

I heard a sound behind me and I looked over my shoulder, then I turned right around.

A woman was standing in the doorway. She was staring curiously at me.

She had Titian red hair: a lot of it, piled to the top of her head, rather sloppily. She was a beauty although her mouth was too big and her lips too thick. There was a sensual quality about her that would attract any man: it attracted me.

She was wearing a crisp white overall, pulled tight around her, and as she moved through the doorway, I could see she hadn't a stitch on under the overall. She was about thirty. She had cold green eyes and her skin was the colour of old ivory.

She didn't say anything. We just stood there, looking at each other. Then Jenson came in, grinning nervously and introduced me.

She nodded at me, still saying nothing: her green eyes hostile.

Jenson stood awkwardly, rubbing his jaw, grinning fatuously at us.

"I guess he could use some food. I know I could," he said finally. "How about it, Lola?"

Her face was expressionless as she said, "I'll get you something."

She turned and walked back into the kitchen.

I could see the outline of her heavy hips under the overall. They rolled sensually as she walked.

42

I picked up a paper napkin and wiped my face. Sweat was running off me.

"Pretty hot, huh?" Jenson said, his grin widening.

"It's hot all right," I said.

My face felt stiff as I tried to match his grin.

II

It was while Jenson and I were unloading the scrap off the truck that he began to talk about his wife.

I had eaten one of the best meals in my life. She had come out of the kitchen carrying two plates loaded with spaghetti and big veal steaks, and had planked them down on the counter and then had gone back into the kitchen without a word.

While we were eating and to ease Jenson's obvious embarrassment I asked him what he wanted me to do now I was going to work for him.

He said he would like me to take care of the garage and the gas pumps so that he and Lola could concentrate on the lunch room. He would like me to do three night shifts every other week and two the alternate week. Any breakdown jobs that came in he expected me to handle, and it would be my job to keep the outside clean and tidy.

"You'll be busy, Jack," he said, "but in this heat and with nothing else to do, it's a good thing to be busy."

I said that was okay with me. I couldn't be busy enough. I meant that. I knew if I started sitting around doing nothing in this place, my mind wouldn't be anywhere else except in the kitchen where she was. She would have that effect on any man.

After we had finished the meal we went outside and he showed me how the gas pumps worked, explained what I had to do when a customer arrived and showed me the tariff of charges for oil and gas.

He then asked me to give him a hand unloading the scrap.

By now the sun was sinking behind the hills and it was cooler. I was glad of the chance to exercise my muscles after being cooped up for so long in the freight truck.

As we worked, he talked.

"You don't have to worry about Lola," he said. "She hates to be crossed. I told you: she's always been against anyone working here. I don't know why. It's just one of those fool ideas women get into their heads." He looked at me anxiously. "You don't want to take it to heart. Maybe for a couple of days she will sulk, but she'll get over it."

I didn't say anything: there didn't seem anything to say.

We hauled a rusty rotary cultivator off the truck. I was impressed by Jenson's strength. He handled the machine as if it were a toy.

As we dragged the machine into the shed, he said, "Don't you think she's a fine looking woman?"

"Yes."

He took out a pack of cigarettes and offered me one. As we lit up, he went on, "Funny thing how we met. Two years ago she got off the Greyhound bus and walked into the lunch room. I was feeling pretty low at the time. My wife had died a couple of weeks back, and I was trying to run this place single handed. I was even trying to do the cooking, and let me tell you, the food was terrible. She asked for a hamburger. Funny how one remembers a thing like that, isn't it? I remember too she was wearing a green dress. The bus stopped for twenty minutes to collect the mail and parcels and give the passengers a chance to get something to eat. They all crowded in: all yelling for sandwiches, pies, hamburgers and so on, and I was swamped. I didn't know whether I was on my head or my heels, then suddenly there she was behind the counter instead of in front of it, serving. I saw she knew the business, and I let her handle the rush. I just showed her where everything was. Before the bus left, everyone was fed. I couldn't have done it myself, but she had done it. I had the same feeling about her as I had about you. I told her if she wanted a job, there was one here for her." He squatted down by the rotary cultivator and began to loosen the gear wire. "Like you, she didn't hesitate. The bus left without her. I gave her the cabin: like I've given it to you. Well, she worked for me for a couple of weeks, then I got thinking." He looked up, his blue eyes guileless. "I knew it wasn't right to have her here alone. People at Wentworth began to talk. When they came here for a snack or for gas, they sniggered at us. They thought things were happening that weren't. So one evening, I talked to her. I asked her if she liked it here: if it wasn't too lonely for her. She said she liked it, so I suggested we got married. That way we'd stop the sniggering and the talk. She would have security, and if anything happened to me, she'd have the place. So we got married." He got the gear wire loose and began to take off the cover of the gearbox. I stood by him, smoking and listening. "Mind you, she's twenty-three years younger than I am," he went on. "I wondered if I was doing right, but she wanted to stay and I couldn't have her here unless we were married. When a man of my age marries a woman as young as she is, he has to have a lot of patience. She'll sulk now for a

44

couple of days, but she'll do her job. One of the great things about her is the way she works: I've never seen anyone work like her."

A car came out of the desert in a whirl of dust and pulled up by the gas pumps. That broke up our conversation. I went out and served my first customer. I gave him gas and oil. I checked his tyres, washed his windshield, and while I worked I was aware Jenson had come to the door of the shed and was watching me.

The guy in the car was fat and elderly. He sat picking his teeth with a match while I worked over his car. I thought I would try a little salesmanship on him.

"Are you going to Tropica Springs, mister?" I asked as I polished his windshield.

"Yeah."

"It'll take you best part of three hours. You won't get in before ten. Aren't you hungry? We serve the best beef hash in the district."

He blinked at me.

"Beef hash?" He looked at his watch. "No, I guess I haven't the time. I'm in a hurry."

"It's ready," I said. "Take you ten minutes, and we do a fruit pie that's really something. I've just had a slice: best pie I've ever tasted."

"Is that right?" He looked interested. "Well, okay. I'll give it a try if it's ready." He got out of the car. "Where do I go?"

I pointed to the lunch room.

"Did you spot the tappet?" I said as he moved off. "It should be fixed. I can do it while you're eating if it's okay with you."

"Sure. I should have had it fixed weeks ago. Thanks."

He went into the lunch room and Jenson, grinning from ear to ear, came over.

"Nice work, Jack. That's what I call salesmanship. I'll give you a hand with the tappet."

While we were working on the car, a black Cadillac slid up to the pumps. I left Jenson to get on with the tappet and went over to the Caddy to serve gas. There was a man and a woman in the car. They looked hot and dusty.

"Can we get a wash here?" the man asked, getting out of the car.

"Sure thing. Round the back to your left. If you're hungry there's veal steaks and spaghetti all ready and waiting. Italian cooking: nothing to touch it, even in Tropica Springs."

The man cocked his eyebrows at me.

"I bet it's old horse and rope."

"I've just had it. I didn't notice any rope in the spaghetti," I

45

said cheerfully. "It was just a suggestion. You won't get to Tropica Springs until past ten. I thought maybe you were hungry."

"I'm starving," the woman said, getting out of the car. "Why not eat here, honey? It can't poison us."

"Okay, if you want to. I could do with something myself."

Ten minutes later, two big Buick Station wagons rolled up with a party of ten. While I was servicing the cars I suggested they might like to eat here and I gave them a lyrical description of the fried chicken. They fell for it.

Jenson had fixed the tappet by now and he went inside to help out with the rush.

A couple of trucks pulled in. The two truckers went into the lunch room for ham and eggs. Then a Jaguar came in with a boy and girl. I told them about the spaghetti and the veal steaks and reminded them how long it would be before they would get a meal unless they eat here. They fell for it too.

Jenson came out, looking worried.

"Jack, the steaks are off and we've only one chicken left," he said. "Go easy on the sales talk."

I stared at him.

"You mean you've run out of food?"

"That's a fact. We don't usually serve more than three or four dinners a night. Usually it's snacks or hamburgers: stuff like that, but with your line of high pressure salesmanship we've got fifteen dinners in there."

"Don't you want them?"

He tapped me on the chest.

"You bet I want them, only I wasn't expecting someone like you to be selling my food. I'll be ready for you tomorrow. Lola and me will go into Wentworth and stock up." He grinned delightedly at me. "There's still plenty of ham and eggs left. See what you can do with those."

He went back into the lunch room.

The truckers started to come in for gas now and the private car trade fell off. I didn't have to sell the truckers food. They knew what they wanted.

Finally, around ten o'clock, the traffic quieted down, and after waiting around for twenty minutes and seeing no headlights coming out of the desert, I went into the lunch room.

There were a couple of truckers eating pie at the counter. Jenson was clearing up and stacking dishes. Someone had fed a coin in the juke-box which was blaring swing.

There was no sign of Lola, but I could hear her clattering dishes in the kitchen.

"Anything I can do?"

Jenson shook his head.

"It's okay. We can manage. You get off to bed. It's my shift tonight. Yours tomorrow." He jerked his head towards the kitchen door and grimaced. "She's still sulking, but she'll get over it. You start tomorrow at eight o'clock. Okay?"

"Sure," I said.

"Come in here for breakfast. And say, Jack, I hope you're as pleased with the job as I am with you."

"I like it a lot," I said, "and I'm glad you're pleased. Well, if I can't do anything, I guess I'll hit the hay."

I went across to the cabin, stripped off and got into bed. I was pretty tired, but my mind was too active for sleep. I kept thinking of Jenson's wife, knowing I shouldn't, but finding it impossible to keep her out of my mind.

The bed was right by the window, and from where I lay, I could look directly across the highway at the bungalow.

I was still trying to sleep an hour later when I saw a light go up in one of the bungalow windows.

I saw her standing in the middle of the room. She was smoking a cigarette, and for some moments she just stood there, letting smoke drift from between her lips. Then moving languidly, she stubbed out the cigarette, dropping the butt on the floor. She pulled out a hairpin and the thick mass of red hair came tumbling down to her waist.

By now I was sitting up, leaning forward and staring; my heart thumping and my breathing was fast. She wasn't more than thirty yards from me.

She sat on a chair in front of the dressing table mirror and began to brush her hair. She spent nearly five minutes stroking the red mass with the brush, then putting the brush down, she crossed over to the bed and turned down the cover.

She moved to the window and began to unfasten her overall. As the overall swung open, she reached out and pulled down the blind. With the light behind her, her shadow was sharp etched against the blind.

She took off the overall, letting it drop to the floor. Her naked silhouette against the blind turned my mouth dry.

Long after she had turned off the light, I still sat at the window, looking across at the bungalow.

It was only when a truck pulled up at the pumps and I saw Jenson come out of the bungalow that I lay down on the bed.

I didn't sleep much that night.

CHAPTER FIVE

I

WHEN I walked into the lunch room at six forty-five the next morning, Lola, clad only in a yellow halter and a pair of scarlet shorts, was scrubbing down the counter.

In that getup, she looked really something. The combination of her red hair, her green eyes and that creamy skin that goes with that colouring, plus her shape the halter and shorts scarcely concealed, had me staring.

She paused in her work to look sulkily at me, then continued to scrub.

"Good morning, Mrs. Jenson," I said. "Can I do that for you?"

Again she paused, her green eyes hostile.

"When I want you to do anything for me I'll tell you," she snapped.

"Why, sure," I said. "I didn't mean any offence."

"If you want breakfast, get it in the kitchen."

She bent over the counter, using the scrub brush. I could see the deep hollow between her breasts.

She looked up.

"What are you staring at?"

"I didn't know I was staring," I lied, and moved around the counter and into the kitchen.

Jenson was sitting at the table. There was a pile of money in bills and small change in front of him. By his side was a cup of coffee, a used plate and a knife and fork. He looked up, nodding at me.

"Come on in, Jack. Do you want ham and eggs?"

"Just coffee," I said, and went over to the pot standing on the hot plate.

"As soon as we've cleared up, Lola and me are going into Wentworth," he said. "We've had the best day for years here. Those fifteen dinners put us right in front. You keep that up, Jack, and I'll be retiring. Just to make it interesting for you, I'm going to give you five per cent on all the restaurant checks. How's that?"

"Why, that's fine, Mr. Jenson. Thanks."

48

"When I'm in Wentworth, I'll get you an overall to work in. Is there anything else you want?"

"I need some clothes, but I guess I'd better get them myself."

"Yeah. You can take the car to Wentworth tomorrow and fit yourself out. I'll give you an advance on your restaurant cut. How about a hundred bucks?"

"That would do fine. Thanks a lot."

He pushed five twenties over to me.

"So tomorrow you go to Wentworth." He leaned back in his chair. "Do you think you could do something with that rotary cultivator? I bought it for scrap, but I have an idea it would still work with a little persuasion."

"I'll take a look at it."

"We'll be off in an hour, but we'll be back by midday. Do you think you can handle it on your own?"

"I don't see why not."

I washed out the coffee cup, then lighting a cigarette, I went into the lunch room.

Lola was putting pies in the glass case and arranging the labels on them. Her back was to me. I paused for a moment, feeling the blood move through me at the sight of her square shoulders, her narrow waist and her heavy hips. She must have known I was staring at her, but she didn't look around.

I went out into the pale sunshine, and taking a broom, I swept up around the gas pumps.

A couple of trucks pulled in for gas. I tried to persuade the truckers to have breakfast but they were in a hurry.

When I was through cleaning up, I went into the shed and inspected the rotary cultivator. On a shelf I found a tin of rust remover and I got to work.

An hour later, Jenson came in.

"We're off now, Jack. Sure you can manage?"

"You bet, Mr. Jenson."

"How's it coming?"

"It wants working on, but it'll be okay."

He rested his heavy hand on my shoulder as he looked at the machine.

"You get the rust off. I'll fix it. See you around midday."

I moved with him to the shed door.

Lola was coming out of the bungalow. She looked smart in a green linen dress. It was a little tight across her chest. Her bust line was something that is now accepted as standard these days, but I wasn't movie trained. Her bust line made me stare.

Jenson gave me a poke in the ribs.

"She looks a real lady, doesn't she? Plenty of style, huh?"

"You're right."

"Yeah, plenty of style. Well, I'll be seeing you."

I watched them drive off in a cloud of dust.

I lit a cigarette and stood looking around. I told myself this was just the kind of place I would like to own. The thought dropped into my mind that Lola was the woman I would like to share it with. I went back to the shed and continued to work on the cultivator. I kept thinking of her in the halter and shorts, and the picture I had of her in my mind made concentration difficult.

I had been working on the cultivator for an hour or so when a car pulled up right outside the shed in which I was working.

It was an old, dusty Chevrolet. A tall, lean man in his middle forties got out of the car, followed by a thin, yellow dog of no particular breed that moved close to the man's heels, its big, blood-shot eyes mournful.

The man wore a pair of faded blue overalls, patched at the knees. Around his scraggy neck was a greasy red handkerchief, knotted at his throat. At the back of his head he wore a high crowned straw hat, burned yellow by the sun.

His face, the colour of teak, was thin and fiddle shaped. He had a long thin nose and thin lips. His eyes, under greying bushy eyebrows, were steady and piercing.

There was something about him I didn't like. He made me think of a cop. Those eyes were prying, suspicious and distrusting.

We looked at each other for a long moment, then I straightened up.

"Something I can do for you?" I said. I had to make a conscious effort to meet those prying eyes.

He leaned against the shed door, his thumbs hooked in the arm straps of his overalls. The dog sat by him, staring fixedly at me.

"Maybe," he said. "Maybe you can tell me who you are and what you are doing here. Maybe you can tell me where Carl Jenson is. Maybe you can tell me to mind my own business."

"Mr. Jenson is in Wentworth with Mrs. Jenson," I said. "I'm Jack Patmore, the new hand."

"Is that a fact?" He shifted his position. "You mean, Carl has hired you to help out?"

"That's right."

"Well, well. I never thought he would do it." He shook his head. All the time his hard little eyes were running over me, taking in my stained, crumpled trousers, my dirty shirt and my scuffed shoes. "Never thought he'd take on help, specially when that wife of his is so set against it." He scratched the side of his face, continuing to shake his head. "I'm his brother-in-law. Ricks is the name—George Ricks."

I guessed he wouldn't be Lola's brother. He must be the late Mrs. Jenson's brother.

So I didn't have to go on meeting those suspicious little eyes, I squatted down beside the rotary cultivator, my back to him.

"You said his wife went with him to Wentworth?" Ricks asked.

"Yes."

"So you're alone here?"

"That's right."

I heard him move forward, and he began to breathe down the back of my neck as I worked on the gearbox.

"I bet Carl bought that as scrap. I bet he got it for a song. Wouldn't surprise me to hear someone paid him to take it away."

I didn't say anything. This man was beginning to get on my nerves.

"Carl's a smart cookie all right," Ricks went on. "He'll look at a lump of rusty iron and see profit in it whereas another guy would just see rusty iron. I bet he'll get that cultivator working again and make a big profit out of it. Yeah, he's smart when it comes to metal, but he's plain dumb when it comes to people."

I made a grunting noise as I got the gear cogs out. I put them in a petrol bath.

"What do you think of that wife of his?"

I was glad I was bending over the machine so he couldn't see my face. I wasn't expecting that one. It jolted me.

"She's all right," I said.

I reached for a screw driver and began to dismantle the clutch plates.

"All right? Is that what you think? I bet she doesn't want you here. She doesn't want anyone here. She doesn't want me here: her husband's brother-in-law. Never thought Carl would be such an old fool as to marry a tramp like her. She walked in here one day from nowhere and going nowhere. She's smart all right. She saw her chance and grabbed it. All she had to do was to wave her sex and her body in front of him, and the dope fell for it. You watch out. Don't kid yourself you'll stay here long because you won't. She'll talk Carl into getting rid of you. Know why?"

By now I had fixed a dumb look on my face. I turned to stare at him.

"I don't know what you're talking about," I said. "I'm just the hired help around here."

He grinned at me, showing big yellow teeth.

"That's right, you told me." He settled himself against the shed door. "She's scared someone will put the bite on Carl. She's after his money. I know. I've watched her. You haven't been around here long enough to get wise to her little tricks. She's after his money: that's all she thinks about. He's been salting money away for years. He has always been a careful man, never spends a dime, although he's generous when he gets the chance, but with that

51

tramp around, watching every move, he doesn't get a chance. Before she came I was welcomed here. There was always a meal here for me, but not now. She sulks when I come. Do you know what happens? She locks her bedroom door. When you're an old fool like Carl, getting on in years, every day counts, and it upsets him if he can't get into the sack with her. That's how she puts the screws on him. If he does anything she doesn't like, the bedroom door gets locked. You watch out. You won't last long. I know her. She'll imagine you are after her money."

I sat back on my heels and examined the clutch plates. One of them was cracked. I put the plates in the petrol bath. Then I stood up and walked over to the work bench to pick up a rag to clean my hands.

He was watching me, but I kept my face dead pan and I could see my apparent indifference irritated him.

"Where have you come from, friend?" he asked abruptly. "Are you a stranger in these parts?"

"That's right."

"How did you run into Carl?"

"I met him in Little Creek."

"You did? Looking for work, huh?"

"That's it."

"Well . . ." He pushed himself away from the shed door. The dog had been sitting motionless: now it stood up. It looked expectantly at Ricks. "I mustn't take up your time. I just looked in to borrow some tools. I've a little job up at my place that needs fixing. I always borrow what I want from Carl." He wandered around the shed, staring at the tool racks. "Now, let me see. What do I want?"

He took down two screw drivers and a hammer. He was reaching for a drill when I said, "I'm sorry, Mr. Ricks, but I can't let you take those tools."

I saw him stiffen, then he looked sideways at me, his thin face expressionless.

"What was that, friend?"

"I haven't Mr. Jenson's permission to let tools go off this place," I said. "I'm responsible here while he's away. If you'll stick around until he comes back and he says it's okay, then it'll be okay, but no tools go out of here without his sayso."

He took the drill out of the rack and then reached for a hacksaw.

"Just relax, friend. I'm his brother-in-law. You're dead right. Anyone else but me shouldn't borrow anything from here—but me, that's different."

I had had enough of this guy.

I walked over to him.

"I'm sorry, Mr. Ricks, no tools go out of here without Mr. Jenson's sayso."

He eyed me. I could see a little red glint come into his eyes. The dog, as if sensing trouble, began to back slowly away.

"Now look, friend," Ricks said, "you don't want to lose your job this soon, do you? If I tell Carl . . ."

"Go ahead and tell him," I said. "Those tools stay here. I'm sorry, but that's the way it is. If you want them that badly you'll have to wait until Mr. Jenson comes back and says you can have them."

"I see." There was sweat on his face now. He looked suddenly as mean as hell. The dog slunk out of the shed and headed for the car. "So there are two of you here now, is that it? You wouldn't also be after his money—like that tramp? Maybe's she's letting you into her sack—is that it?"

I felt a rush of blood to my head. I caught hold of his overall and gave him a shake that nearly snapped his head off his shoulders, then I shoved him away from me.

"Get out of here!" I said. "Hear me? Beat it!"

He nearly fell over himself backing away. His face had gone yellow-green under his tan and his eyes popped out of his mean, thin face.

"I'll fix you for this!" he quavered. "I'll tell Carl . . ."

"Get out!"

He turned and walked fast to his car. The dog was already in it. Ricks got into the car, slammed the door and drove off in a cloud of dust.

I was worried. I didn't know how Jenson would react if Ricks complained. At least I would get my story in first, but I wasn't going to tell Jenson what Ricks had said about his wife. I was pretty sure Jenson wouldn't like that part of it, coming from me.

When they got back around midday and while I was helping Jenson unload the estate wagon, I told him Ricks had been here and had tried to borrow tools.

"I had to get a little rough with him, Mr. Jenson. He wouldn't take no for an answer. I chased him out. If I did wrong, I'm sorry."

Jenson grinned at me.

"You did absolutely right. I should have warned you about him. That guy drives me crazy. I won't let him take a thing off the place. One time I used to, but I never got anything back. He's the biggest scrounger in the district. When my first wife was alive, he was never off the place. He came in for every meal, filled his car with my gas, borrowed my tools, borrowed money from my wife —he drove me nuts. After I married Lola, she fixed him. I haven't

53

seen him now for a couple of months, but he'll turn up again. Don't let him have a thing if I'm not here."

I was relieved I hadn't made a mistake so far as Jenson was concerned, but I had an idea I had made a mistake so far as Ricks was concerned.

I told myself I would have to watch out for him. He could mean trouble for me.

II

Three weeks can seem a long time.

With the sun coming up behind the distant mountain, turning the desolate desert into a crimson wasteland, and as I lay in my bed, looking out of the window, I thought back on the three weeks I had now been at Point of No Return.

I now had a feeling of security. Farnworth, its stinking bunkhouse and its brutal guards seemed a remote nightmare: something that had never happened. I no longer felt a twinge of fear every time a car came out of the heat haze and pulled up beside the gas pumps. I was fairly certain now that I had become a lost man to the police, and if I continued to stay out here in this lonely place, I would remain safe.

Although Lola still didn't speak to me unless she could help it, she now seemed resigned to me. I still found her disturbing and sensually attractive, but that didn't mean I even thought about doing anything about it.

I had too much respect and too much liking for Jenson. I had known from the start that he was my kind of people, but as the days went by, and we worked long hours together, I found he was something a lot more than that. He was a man you just had to like: a simple guy with a kindness in his heart that made you react to him unless you were a sonofabitch like George Ricks.

Jenson and I got along fine together. I soon found that although he was crazy about Lola, he yearned for male company. He liked to play gin rummy in the evenings while we waited for the late customer. He liked to talk about his past life and his ambitions, and from what I could see neither of these pastimes interested Lola. I played a good game of gin and I was happy to let him talk.

I soon discovered he was shrewd and smart. He had a surprising talent for turning rusty scrap into something he could sell at a profit. He had put the rotary cultivator in order and had sold it to a farmer for a hundred and fifty dollars.

He was like a kid with excitement when he had pulled off the sale.

"That's a hundred and thirty bucks profit, Jack," he said, grinning from ear to ear. "That's what I call a deal."

Then one night when we had finished a game of gin, and Lola had gone to bed, and we two were sitting on the veranda of the lunch room, waiting for some trade, he suddenly got confidential.

"Know what I plan to do in a couple of years, Jack?" he said, stretching out his massive legs and getting out his pipe. "I plan to go right around the world. It'll take three years to do the job properly. When I'm ready, I'm going to sell this place, then me and Lola are going. Right the way around the world, missing nothing. First class all the way: the best hotels, everything arranged and taken care of."

I stared at him.

"That's going to cost a whale of a lot of money," I said.

"Yeah." He paused to light his pipe, then went on. "I've got the price all worked out. It's going to hit me for sixty thousand bucks. On top of that there's clothes, drinks and spending money. I reckon it'll cost at least a hundred thousand. Well, I've got it, Jack. I've been saving for the past thirty years, and I've got it. I want to put by some capital to make a fresh start when I come back. I'll have what I want in a couple of years, then away we go."

"You mean you've really got a hundred thousand dollars, Mr. Jenson?"

"Yes." He winked broadly at me. "I've got a system, Jack. I wouldn't tell anyone this, but you and me are pals, and I know it won't go any further. For thirty years, I've been making nice money out of scrap. It's just one of those things. I guess I have a talent for it. It has been cash right down the line, and with cash, the tax inspector doesn't come into it. I've kept two sets of books for years. In one of them I've logged the gas sales and the lunch room sales: that's for the tax inspector. In the other book I've kept a record of my scrap sales, and that's for me. That book tells me I've cleaned up one hundred thousand bucks."

"Out of scrap?"

"Yeah. It wouldn't be anything like that if the money had been taxed, but the way I've worked it, the tax man isn't smelling a dime of it. It's for Lola and me and the world trip."

I suddenly remembered what Ricks had said about Lola marrying Jenson for his money.

"Does she know about it?" I asked.

"Sure, she knows about it, but she doesn't know what I plan to do with it. In another year, when I'm ready to quit, I'll tell her. It'll be a real surprise for her. Imagine! A trip around the world!"

On this particular morning, two days after this conversation, and three weeks since I had come to Point of No Return, I lay in bed, brooding about Lola.

It was her turn for night shift, and from time to time during the night I had heard trucks pulling up and I had looked out of the window to see her in jeans and a shirt serving gas and talking to the truckers.

Jenson had wanted her to give up the night shift now I was there to help out, but she wouldn't. She said she liked doing it. She knew most of the truckers, and they liked her. So Jenson reluctantly let her do one shift a week. He did two and I did four.

After one o'clock in the morning the traffic dropped away, and the one on nightshift could then turn in. It was seldom anyone came after that hour, and if they did, there was a night bell to ring.

I watched Lola as she sat in the basket chair on the veranda preparing string beans for the lunch trade. The time was just after six.

I saw the grocery truck coming. It came regularly every morning, bringing the groceries and any special orders from Wentworth. As the driver pulled up outside the lunch room, I tossed off the sheet and got out of bed.

The guy carried the big box of provisions up the steps and into the lunch room, and Lola followed him.

I stretched and yawned, then wandered into the bathroom. I was feeling relaxed and pretty good. As I let the cold water from the shower run over me, I thought of Farnworth. I couldn't help feeling complacent. I had certainly had some luck, but at the same time I had been pretty smart the way I had handled my escape.

But my luck was running out, although I didn't know it right then. In that box of provisions the guy had just carried into the lunch room was something that was going to blow my complacency and my feeling of security sky high.

One of Fate's little jokes.

This day was pay day.

With a roll of money in his big sweating hand, Jenson came lumbering into the shed where I was working after breakfast on the wreck of an outboard motor he had been paid to take away.

"How's it coming, Jack?" he said, standing over me. "Think you can fix it?"

I looked up and grinned at him.

"Why, sure," I said. "I'll get it to work, but I don't guarantee how long it will last. This one's a bad one: pretty nearly played out, but I'll get it to work."

"Good boy." He wagged his head at me. "We'll make a few

bucks out of it, huh? I've got some dough for you. Forty for the job—right?"

"Yeah."

"Then there's the restaurant cut: a hundred and ten."

"As much as that?"

He laughed.

"Hear the man talk! You've sold more lunches and more dinners than we've ever sold before. You're a knock out! Just as a sign of appreciation, I'm giving you another hundred for the scrap you've worked on."

I stared at him.

"I didn't expect that, Mr. Jenson. After all, this is my job."

"Now look, Jack, leave this to me. You're doing all right. It was my lucky day when you came here. Since you've been here I've made a stack of dough. Take what I'm giving you and shut up."

"If that's the way you feel—well, thanks." I took the bundle of bills he thrust at me. "Now you have me worried. I'm not spending the money I'm earning. I have it all in my cabin. With what you have just given me, I have over five hundred dollars. So what do I do with it? Would you give me an introduction to your bank?"

"My bank?" He laughed, shaking his head. "Who wants to put their money in a bank? Three years ago the Wentworth bank failed. All the guys who had put their savings in that bank went under. I don't trust banks. I've never given any bank a cent of mine. I like it in cash. I like to know if anything happened to me, Lola could put her hands on my money without a lot of talk from the bank. Okay, you have five hundred dollars. I'll take care of it for you. I have a safe. That's where I keep my money. I'll keep yours with mine. Then when you want to spend it, you come to me and you'll get it in cash. Cash is more important than any bank talk. Never mind about putting the money out at interest. You can lose plenty of money if you're after interest. One day it's up, the next day it's down, and if you want your money quick, you're always out on the deal. You make a note of what you've got. I'll keep it for you, then any time you want it, you can put your hands on it."

I stood up, gaping at him.

"You don't keep your hundred thousand dollars in a safe here, do you?" I said.

"Why, of course I do. Why not? You don't imagine I'd trust any bank around here to keep that amount of money for me? I've a safe that's really good—the best. A Lawrence safe is the best money can buy. I don't have to tell you that. You know safes. Isn't that right? Isn't a Lawrence safe the best money can buy?"

"Is that what you've got?"

"Why, sure. I had a salesman out here some five years ago. He sold me this safe. He was the sincerest salesman I've ever known. Put money in a Lawrence and it's safe. That's what he told me—that's the Corporation's slogan, and a damn good one too. He was right, wasn't he, Jack?"

That sardine can? That box of phoney steel I could open in three minutes?

I looked at his beaming face and I saw how proud he was of his judgment. I hadn't the heart to tell him.

"Why, sure. I know them. They're the best."

He reached out and patted my shoulder. I was getting used to his pats now, but each time he dropped his great hand on my shoulder my knees sagged. He just didn't know his own strength.

"Okay, then I'll keep your money for you. Any time you want it . . . just say the word."

"Well, thanks, Mr. Jenson."

"Go and get it. I'll give you a receipt. May as well make it safe right now. You never know. Keeping it in your cabin's no good. Who knows? The cabin may burn down."

So like a dope, I went over to the cabin and took the money I had saved from under my mattress and gave it to him. He gave me a receipt for five hundred and ten dollars.

"I'll lock it up right away, Jack," he said, and I could see he was as pleased as he could be. "Any time you want it . . ."

"Sure," I said.

He looked at his watch.

"Moving up for twelve. We have the Greyhound bus here at half-past. That'll mean thirty people. Suppose you give Lola a hand? I'll put your money away, then I'll take care of the pumps. In half an hour we're going to be busy."

"Right," I said.

I went over to the lunch room and into trouble.

Lola was arranging newly-baked pies in the glass case as I walked in. She looked over her shoulder at me.

There was an expression in her green eyes that immediately warned me that something was up.

"Anything I can do to help out?" I said.

She smiled. This was the first time she had smiled at me: a jeering smile that started an alarm bell ringing in my head.

"There's plenty for you to do, *Patmore*," she said. The emphasis she put on the phoney name I had given myself sent up the red light. "I've unpacked the groceries—suppose you put them away?"

I went into the kitchen. The cans of food, the two dozen chickens in their plastic bags and rest of the stuff were spread out on two tables.

COME EASY — GO EASY

Lying on the cans of food was a crumpled newspaper that had obviously been used to pack something in. I picked it up. Then my heart gave a violent kick against my side.

Don't ask me how a Wentworth grocery store had got hold of an Oakland local newspaper. That's one of the jokes of life, but there it was: the front page of the *Oakland Inquirer,* and slap on the front page was my photograph with a banner headline:

ESCAPED SAFE ROBBER STILL FREE.

I stood motionless, staring at the photograph, feeling cold chills running through me. It wasn't a good photograph, but good enough, and she had pencilled in my moustache on the photograph to tell me that she knew who I was.

Farnworth, the stinking bunk-house and the brutal guards suddenly came into focus. They were no longer a remote nightmare.

In the silence of the safe, clean kitchen, I heard the screams of a man in the punishment cell and the hissing crack of the belts as the guards beat him. I saw again the guy who had lost an eye, staggering down the corridor, his shirt and trousers plastered to his back with blood, his hands covering his face.

My dream of safety dissolved the way a fist disappears when you open your hand.

Had she told Jenson? I was pretty sure she hadn't yet. If she had I would have known by his manner. But she was certain to. This was the perfect excuse for getting rid of me.

All she had to do was to reach out for the telephone, and I'd be on my way back to Farnworth within the hour.

I could imagine the welcome I would get there. I could imagine the gleeful, sadistic grins of the prisoners as I was marched across the tarmac to the Chief's office. I could imagine them, listening and nudging each other, as they waited for my first yell of pain.

I crumpled the newspaper between my hands, then I went over to the stove and dropped it in.

So I was on the run again. I had to get out of here. But how? I was one hundred and sixty-five miles from Tropica Springs. Once she had told them I had been here, Tropica Springs would be the first place they would look for me. I didn't dare double back to Oakland. I would have to get to Tropica Springs and then go on from there. At least I had five hundred dollars. With that money I could take a plane to New York . . . five hundred dollars? I felt cold fingers squeezing my heart. I had given my getaway stake to Jenson not half an hour ago! Now I would have to ask him for it! What would he think? Anyway, how could I walk out of here in daylight without him thinking I had gone nuts?

I was in such a panic I could scarcely breathe.

Then the kitchen door swung open and she came in.

59

She looked at me: a searching, jeering, probing expression in her green eyes.

"Haven't you put the groceries away yet?" she said.

"I'm putting them away."

I began to pick up some of the cans.

You bitch! I was thinking. Have you called the police? What have you done?

She began to put the chickens in the freezer. She hummed under her breath as she worked.

It wasn't until I had put the groceries in the cupboard and she had packed the last chicken into the freezer that she said suddenly, "It's time you and I had a talk. It's your night shift to-night, isn't it?"

I faced her. "Yes."

"When he's asleep I'll talk to you."

That told me she hadn't called the police. She was going to make terms. I began to breathe again.

"Anything you say."

"Run away, Mr. Chet Carson," she said. "I can manage very well without you."

Well, there it was. She had me over a barrel, but at least I had a little time before the axe fell.

I looked her over: aware of her body under the halter and the shorts.

"Anything you say."

She smiled.

"That's right, Carson. From now on—it's going to be anything I say."

As I walked out into the lunch room, the Greyhound bus arrived and from it spilled thirty hungry customers.

The three of us slaved. Jenson and I handled the lunch room. Lola slogged in the kitchen. Every one of the passengers took the lunch. When I wasn't handing around the lunches, I was rushing out to serve gas.

I'll say this for Lola: the way she kept the food moving out of the kitchen was really something. No one had to wait. Everyone had what they wanted.

Finally, when the bus moved off, we were all pretty bushed.

Jenson grinned at me as he mopped his face.

"This is a record, Jack," he said. "We've never done this before. Without you we would never have made it. Thirty lunches! Before—they had to do with a snack."

"It was the cook," I said.

"Yeah! What a wife! Well, anyway, we three made it. Now look, Lola and me will fix the dishes. You sit out here and take

COME EASY — GO EASY

care of the pumps. You've got the night shift. No point in killing yourself."

In an ordinary way, I would have done my stint, but I couldn't face working close to her. I wanted time off to think. Now the rush was over, I had the bile of fear in my mouth again.

When he had gone into the lunch room, I sat down and lit a cigarette. I was just starting to relax when I felt someone watching me.

I looked over my shoulder.

Lola had come out onto the veranda. She was staring at me: her green eyes glittering.

Jenson had come to the open window, a stack of dishes in his hands. He looked worried.

"What's this patsy think he's doing?" Lola shrilled. "Doesn't he work here any more? Have I got to do all the work?"

"Look, honey," Jenson said pleadingly, "he's on night shift . . ."

"I don't give a damn what he's on." To me, she said, "Go in and clear the dishes! If anyone is going to loll around in a chair it's going to be me! Now get in there and earn what we're paying you."

"Hey, Lola!" Jenson said, his voice sharpening.

I was on my feet and moving towards her.

"I'm sorry, Mrs. Jenson: just as you say."

"Lola! Quit talking to the guy like that! I told him to take care of the pumps," Jenson said, leaning half out of the window.

"Don't I get any consideration around here?" she screamed at him. "It seems I'm good only for slaving in a stinking hot kitchen and going to bed with you!"

She ran off past me and over to the bungalow. She went inside and slammed the front door.

Jenson put down the dishes and came out. He looked bad: his face sagging.

"She's worked herself into the ground," I said. "She's tired. Women get like that. They blow off. It doesn't mean a thing. Tomorrow she'll be fine."

He rubbed his jaw, shaking his head and frowning.

"You think so, Jack? I've never heard her speak like that before. You think I should talk to her: soothe her or something?"

I couldn't tell him the whole thing had been an act. She was making sure she would sleep alone this night so when he was asleep she could come out and talk to me.

"I'd leave her alone, Mr. Jenson. It's my bet tomorrow she'll be okay. She's tired. How about you and me fixing these dishes?"

He put his arm around my shoulders.

"You're a good guy, Jack. Most guys would have blown their top to be spoken to the way she spoke to you. I was ashamed. Like

61

you said—she's tired. I'll talk to her about it tomorrow. She doesn't seem to realise what a help you are around here."

"Forget it," I said. "Let's get to work."

It took us until after seven o'clock to clear up the kitchen, what with serving gas, serving snacks and a couple of repairs that came in. There was no sign of Lola until past four o'clock, then as I heard a car engine, I looked out of the window. She was driving off in the Mercury, wearing her green dress. The car was heading for Wentworth.

That scared me. Was she going to the police?

I told Jenson.

He grimaced.

"She's done this before when we've had words. She always goes to the movies. She's crazy about the movies. She won't be back now until after eleven. Well, we'll have to manage on our own, Jack. Can you cook?"

"Why not?" I said. "Anyway, I can fix chickens."

It was while I was preparing the chickens and he was cutting sandwiches that he let drop the hint that he wasn't all that happy with Lola.

"Of course she's young," he said, slicing away at the loaf. "My first wife was different. She and me went to the same school together. We grew up together. She was my age when she died. This one's wild. I'm not saying she doesn't work—she does. She works like hell, but Emmie—that's my first wife—would never have spoken to you the way Lola did just now. She would never have driven off like that without a word. Sometimes I wonder if I shouldn't be tougher with her. Sometimes I'm tempted to smack her behind when she hits the roof. Maybe I should."

As dangerous as slapping a rattlesnake, I thought, but I didn't say so.

"I've often wondered where she came from. She never would tell me. She's hard, Jack. She must have had a pretty hard life. It worries me, too, the way she goes into Wentworth on her own. When you came, I planned she and me could do a movie once or twice a week, but she won't go with me. When I suggest it, she has a headache or she's too tired. I sometimes wonder . . ." He broke off, shaking his head. He walked heavy footed to the cupboard to get more butter.

"You wonder what?" I said, feeling sorry for him.

"Never mind." He began buttering the bread. "I guess I'm talking too much."

I let it go, but I had an idea what he was wondering about. He was wondering if she had found some guy younger than himself. He was wondering if she were cheating.

Around eleven o'clock the traffic fell away. Jenson and I had run the lunch room together. My fried chicken had been a success. We had served ten dinners which wasn't bad. At eleven-fifteen the Mercury pulled up outside the bungalow and Lola got out.

She went straight in and we heard her bedroom door slam.

Jenson shook his head.

"Maybe I'd better talk to her."

"I'd leave it," I said. "She'll be okay tomorrow."

"Well, okay. Maybe you're right." He still looked worried. "I guess I'll turn in. We're all clear now, aren't we?"

"Everything's fine," I said. "Goodnight, Mr. Jenson."

"Goodnight, Jack."

I watched him cross to the bungalow. The light in her room was on, but it snapped out as he opened the front door. The light in his room, which was next to hers, went on.

I came out onto the lunch room veranda and sat down in one of the basket chairs. I was feeling scared, worried sick and tired. I lit a cigarette and settled down to wait. I knew she wouldn't come out here for some time: I had a long wait ahead of me.

I imagined her in her dark bedroom, waiting for Jenson to go to sleep. I wondered what she was thinking about and what she was planning.

If I had had my money, instead of giving it to Jenson to take care of, I would have cleared out now. I would have bribed the first trucker to come in for gas to take me into Tropica Springs. But without money, I was sunk.

So I sat in the darkness, watching the bungalow and waiting for her to come.

CHAPTER SIX

I

THE hands of my wrist watch showed one-forty. For the past half-hour there had been no trucks coming through. I had been sweating it out for over three hours—waiting for her.

Then suddenly I saw her come out of the bungalow. She moved languidly. She was wearing a white shirt and a full, light coloured skirt. Tight at the waist and flowing out over her hips. She was certainly dressed for the occasion.

I was sitting in the basket chair in the shadows and I watched her come, my heart thumping. I had a cigarette between my lips. So she could tell where I was, I drew on the cigarette, making a little red spark in the darkness.

She came slowly up the steps and sat down in a basket chair near mine.

"Give me a cigarette," she said.

I handed her my pack and my lighter. I couldn't bring myself to light her cigarette. I wasn't going to be that much of a slave to her.

She lit her cigarette, then returned me the pack and the lighter. Her fingers brushed mine. They felt hot and dry.

"You puzzled me," she said. "I was sure you were a phoney, but I didn't guess you were the escaped safe robber. You're quite a celebrity."

"What's it to you who I am so long as I do my job and make money for your husband? Why should you care?"

"I have to think of myself." She stretched out her long legs, sinking deeper into the basket chair. "I could get into trouble with the police unless I tell them you're here."

"Are you going to tell them?"

"I haven't decided yet." She drew on the cigarette. After a long pause, she went on, "It depends on you. They said in the newspaper that you worked for Lawrence Safes."

I looked in her direction. I couldn't see her face. She was sitting in the shadows.

"What's that got to do with it?"

"Everything so far as I'm concerned. Carl has a Lawrence safe.
I want you to open it."

So Ricks had been right. She was after Jenson's money.

"Is there something in it that you want?" I said. "Why don't
you ask him for it?"

"Don't be funny!" She moved irritably. "Remember what I
said this afternoon: from now on, you're going to do what I say
or else . . ."

"Doesn't he give you enough? What do you want to steal his
money for?"

"If you don't open the safe, you'll go back to Farnworth." She
crossed her legs, adjusting her skirt. "I've heard about that jail.
They're tough there. They'll know what to do with you once
they get their hands on you. Are you going to open the safe or are
you going back to Farnworth?"

"So Ricks was right. You are a tramp and you are after your
husband's money."

"Never mind what Ricks said. Are you going to open the safe?"

"Suppose I do open it—what happens then?"

"I'll give you a thousand dollars and a twenty-four hour start
to get away."

She had certainly dreamed up a nice little plot. I opened the
safe. She collected a hundred thousand dollars. She gave me a
thousand and I went on the run. Jenson would find the safe empty
and I would be missing. The finger would point to me. Once the
police had my description, they would know I had opened the
safe and they would automatically jump to the conclusion that I
had the money. It would never occur to anyone to suspect her. All
she would have to do was to hide the money somewhere and wait.
If they caught me and I told them she had forced me to open the
safe and she had the money, it would be my word against hers.
Jenson was too crazy about her to believe me. When the uproar
had quietened down, she would take the money and disappear. It
was a sweet little plot, and it could succeed.

"Do you know what he plans to do with the money you want to
steal?" I said, looking towards her. I couldn't see much of her:
just two hostile voices talking in the dark. "He plans to go on a
trip around the world. It's something he has been saving for for
thirty years and he plans to take you with him: everything first
class. Don't you want to go on a trip around the world?"

"With him? With that fat, old fool?" The note in her voice
was vicious. "I don't even want to go to Wentworth with him."

"But he loves you. Did you marry him only for what you could
steal from him?"

"Oh, shut up! How long will it take you to open the safe?"

"I don't know. Maybe I won't be able to open it. Those safes are tough. Without the combination, it's practically impossible to open them."

"You'd better open this one, Carson!"

I was talking to gain time. She had me over a barrel. There wasn't a Lawrence safe made that I couldn't open. But I hated the thought of Jenson losing his money. I hated the thought, too, that for the rest of his days he would believe I had taken it. He was my friend. He was the only friend I had. I couldn't do this to him after what he had done for me, but unless I did I would go back to Farnworth and that was something I just couldn't face. I had to think of a way to get out of this: there had to be a way.

With my mind still busy, I asked, "Where's the safe?"

"In the sitting-room in the bungalow."

"How do you expect me to open it without him hearing me?"

"He's going to a Legion meeting on Saturday. That's when you'll do it."

I flicked the butt of my cigarette out into the hot night. As I lit another, I said, "And what are you supposed to be doing while I'm busting open the safe—watching me?"

"It's my night shift. I'll be in the kitchen, baking pies. I'll be so busy I won't hear you leave. I won't even know you have gone until he gets back."

Then I saw how I could fix her. It was easy. There was nothing to it, except I would be on the run again and I would be out of a good job, but at least I wouldn't have let Jenson down, and that was something pretty important to me.

"What time does he leave and what time will he be back?"

"He leaves at seven and gets back around two o'clock."

All right, you bitch, I said to myself, now I've got it fixed. You are in for a surprise. Okay, I'll open the safe. Then when you walk in to collect, you'll walk into a clip on the jaw. I'll take the money. By the time you've come to, I'll be halfway over the mountain. I'll take care you can't use the telephone and I'll make sure you can't raise the alarm until he gets back and finds you. Then when I'm far away, I'll write to him and tell him the whole story and I'll send him back his money: every cent of it. If I do that, he'll believe me. He'll have to believe me if I do that and he'll know what a treacherous bitch he's married to.

Just to kid her along, I said, "I hate doing a thing like this to him. He's been pretty good to me."

"Never mind the sob talk," she said impatiently. "Are you going to open the safe or are you going back to Farnworth?"

"Well . . ." I paused, then went on, "I'm not going back to Farnworth."

"Then Saturday?"

I pretended to hesitate, then shrugging my shoulders, I said, "I guess so. Okay, I'll do it."

She got to her feet and flicked her cigarette away into the darkness.

"Don't imagine I'm bluffing, Mr. Chet Carson. If you don't open that safe, you're going back to Farnworth."

"You don't have to drive it into the ground," I said, looking up at her. "I said I'd do it, didn't I?"

"You'd better do it!" she said, and walked down the steps across the moonlit sand towards the bungalow.

I watched her go.

Well, the cards were face up on the table. It depended now on who outsmarted who.

I was pretty confident I had the four aces against her four kings.

II

On the following morning, while I was clearing up after the lunch-hour and when Jenson was minding the pumps, I said to Lola, "Get me the number of the safe. I've got to have it before I can handle it."

She looked sideways at me out of her hard green eyes.

"I'll get it."

Later in the day, when Jenson was out of the way, she gave me a slip of paper.

The safe number told me Jenson had been sold an obsolete model which was now off the market. It hadn't been a success because when the safe door was shut it locked automatically. Most safe users preferred to lock the door with a key, and besides, this model had proved to be one of the easiest safes to break into.

It suited me. It wouldn't take me ten minutes to open, and time was an important factor in this set-up.

On Thursday, when Jenson and I were working together in the garage, he said, "I've to go to Wentworth on Saturday night: there's a Legion meeting on. Lola is on night shift. I'll be glad if you'll keep an eye open just in case she runs into a trucker who doesn't know his manners."

I got a tight feeling in my chest.

Jenson trusted me. He was leaving his wife here alone with me and he wanted me to look after her in case some trucker got fresh. It didn't cross his mind that, being alone with her, I might get the same idea.

"I'll watch it, Mr. Jenson," I said. "You don't have to worry."

He grinned at me.

"I know that, Jack. When it comes to men, I don't make mistakes. You're all right."

Friday was my day off. I asked Jenson if I could borrow the Mercury.

"I thought I'd take a look at Tropica Springs."

"You go ahead: sure, take the car."

"I could do with some money. Let me have a hundred, will you, Mr. Jenson?"

"I'll get it right away." I could see he was a little surprised I was asking for so much, and again I cursed myself for letting him handle my savings.

He went off to the bungalow, and after a while he came back with the money.

I asked him if there was anything I could get him in Tropica Springs. He said no, and then gave me a nudge in the ribs.

"Keep away from the cat houses, Jack, and don't come home drunk."

As I drove off, I saw Lola watching me from the kitchen.

You would look a damn sight more sulky, you chippy, I thought, if you knew what I was cooking up for you.

The road over the mountain was tricky with a lot of hairpin bends, and although I kept pressing, it took me close on four hours to reach Tropica Springs. That worried me. It cut my escape time down.

I had my escape plan pretty well organised. I had decided against taking a plane. The airport would be the first place the police would check, and besides, it was unlikely there would be a plane to New York at that hour of the morning.

Parking the car, I went to a travel bureau and inquired the time of trains leaving for New York. I was told there was one leaving Tropica Springs at 12.30 a.m.

As Jenson was leaving for Wentworth at seven, I could get the safe open and the money packed by seven-thirty and could be on my way to Tropica Springs by seven-forty-five. It would only take me a few minutes to fix Lola. That gave me threequarters of an hour to get the train.

Leaving the travel bureau, I went to a nearby store and bought myself a pair of fawn-coloured trousers and a sports coat in grey with big green pouch pockets: the kind of coat you can see coming a half a mile off. I bought a nigger brown straw hat with a red band and a pair of moccasin shoes. I also bought a big suitcase in which I put the clothes. I locked the suitcase in the trunk of the Mercury, then I went to a chemist shop and bought a pair of sun goggles and a bottle of hair bleach. These, too, I locked in the trunk.

Lola would give a description of me to the police: she would tell them what I was wearing, and it was essential to have a complete change of clothing as unlike what I would wear when I left Point of No Return as possible, and to make the change before I reached Tropica Springs.

Satisfied that I had taken care of everything, I drove out of Tropica Springs and headed for Point of No Return.

At the end of the mountain road just as I came out into the desert there was a big patch of scrub and prickly cactus. I stopped the car by it, and taking the suitcase from the trunk, I set it down in the middle of the scrub.

I could easily find it again, and the chances of anyone else finding it was remote enough not to bother me.

I got back to Point of No Return soon after seven, in time to help with the dinner hour. We served eighteen dinners, and we were all kept on the go until eleven o'clock.

It was my night shift, and Jenson went off to bed soon after eleven, leaving me to look after the pumps and Lola to finish up in the kitchen.

Around eleven-thirty, as I sat in the basket chair by the pumps, smoking and looking at the evening paper, Lola came over to me.

"What were you doing in Tropica Springs?" she asked, pausing by me.

"What do you imagine I was doing?" I said, staring at her. "I went out there to book a seat on a plane for San Francisco."

"Is that where you are going?"

"Why should you care where I'm going?"

She lifted her shoulders indifferently.

"I don't: so long as you open the safe."

"I'll open it."

"Yes, you'll open it," she said, and walked away towards the bungalow.

I leaned back in the chair and looked the place over. One more day, and then I would never see it again. I had grown to love it. I took as much pride in it as Jenson did. I was going to miss him too.

For the rest of the night I sat and brooded. I felt depressed. I wondered what I would be doing in a week's time. It was a joke to think I would have a suitcase crammed full of money that didn't belong to me, and which I was determined to send back to Jenson. With that kind of money I could go anywhere and do anything. I could buy a place like this somewhere on the Florida coast, get married and settle down in comfort and safety for the rest of my days.

But I couldn't do it to Jenson: not after the way he had treated me. I had to send the money back to him. I could never live with myself if I didn't.

Around six o'clock on Saturday evening, Jenson came out of the lunch room and joined me in the garage where I was working on the outboard motor.

"Going to wash now, Jack. You okay?"

"All fixed, Mr. Jenson."

"I don't reckon I'll get back much before two o'clock," he said. "These Legion shindigs get a little wild after the business end of it." He winked at me. "Don't tell Lola that."

"You have a good time," I said. I couldn't dig up a smile for him, I was feeling too bad. In an hour he would walk out of my life and I would never see him again.

When he had gone, I went over to the station wagon we used to collect anything too heavy for the Mercury and not heavy enough for the truck. I made sure the gas tank was full and I checked the oil. It was in the station wagon I was going to make my getaway.

For the next twenty minutes we had a stream of cars going through Tropica Springs and I was kept busy. I didn't encourage any of the drivers to stop off for a meal. As soon as Jenson had gone, I wanted to get at the safe.

There was no sign of Lola, but I could hear her clattering dishes in the kitchen. Around five minutes to seven, Jenson came out of the bungalow. He was wearing his best suit and he had a cigar clenched between his teeth. He looked pretty good. He went into the lunch room to say goodbye to Lola.

I was getting the jitters now. I wished he would go so I could tackle the safe. This hanging around was tearing my nerves to shreds.

Finally, just after seven, he came out and I joined him in the Mercury.

"Well, have a good time," I said, looking at him and thinking this was the last time I would see him.

"Take care of things here, Jack. I don't really want to go, but you know how it is."

"Sure. You don't have to worry your head. Mrs. Jenson and I will handle it."

"Yeah." He got into the Mercury.

I would have liked to have shaken his hand. Instead, I could only give him a casual wave.

The evening sun was just beginning to sink behind the mountain: in another half-hour it would be dark.

"So long, Jack."

"So long, Mr. Jenson."

I watched the Mercury drive off in a cloud of dust. I stood there until I had lost sight of it as it entered the foothills, then I started towards the bungalow.

Lola was already there, waiting at the door. She looked pale and her eyes were glittering.

"Where is it?" I said as I joined her.

"In the sitting-room behind the sofa."

"You'd better stay by the pumps," I said. "It'll take me a couple of hours to open."

I saw suspicion jump into her eyes.

"As long as that?"

"I told you, these safes are tough. I haven't the combination. It'll take at least two hours. Get out there and take care of the pumps."

I went into the sitting-room and looked at the safe. It was a combination job with no lock and key.

She stood in the doorway watching me.

"I'll get some tools. Hadn't we better shut the lunch room? You don't want a party coming in and yelling for food."

"I've shut it," she said.

I went past her and across to the garage. I collected some tools and put them in a big canvas bag. The bag would do to carry the money when I got at it. As I came out of the garage I saw a Packard coming fast along the desert road.

Lola saw it too, and she left the front entrance of the bungalow and went over to the pumps. I started for the bungalow as the Packard pulled up.

I glanced at the two men in the car and I felt a cold chill snake up my spine.

They were cops. Although in plain clothes, there was no mistaking them: two big, hard-faced men with aggressive jaws and cold alert eyes.

I kept going, feeling sweat break out all over me.

A voice bawled, "Hey! You!"

I stopped and turned.

Both men got out of the car. Both of them were looking at me.

Lola was staring at them. She knew what they were. She was as tense as I was.

I walked slowly over to them, fighting down my rising panic.

"I've got a flat," the bigger of the two said. "It's in the trunk. Fix it, will you? I don't want to go over the mountain without a spare."

"Why, sure," I said, and taking the key he offered me I went around to the trunk and opened it.

The other cop said to Lola, "Fill her up, sister, and how about some food while the flat's being fixed?"

I saw Lola hesitate. She hadn't the nerve to refuse them.

"Sandwiches okay?" she asked.

"Yeah. Hurry it up. We're late already."

I pulled the tyre out of the trunk and trundled it into the repair shed. It had never been off the rim and it took me twenty minutes to get it off. By then sweat was streaming off me. My escape time was running out. It took me another twenty minutes to repair the flat. While I worked the cops ate sandwiches and drank beer.

It was ten minutes past eight by the time I had fixed the tyre and put it back into the trunk. By that time I should have been on the mountain road, heading for Tropica Springs. It looked now as if I wasn't going to make the New York train.

As the two cops drove away, two cars, loaded with a bunch on vacation, pulled up. All of them yelled for food and wouldn't take no for an answer.

I said to Lola, "It isn't going to work out. We'll have to try some other time. I thought all along this was a cockeyed idea. The timing is wrong."

She gave me a stony look, then went to the lunch room and opened up. The timing was wrong.

For the next two hours we worked like galley slaves. Cars came in in a steady stream: everyone wanted food. It wasn't until ten o'clock that the traffic dropped off.

Both of us were sweating and tired. The night was oven hot: the hottest night I had known out here.

We stood together in the lunch room, looking around at the pile of dishes, the trays of used glasses, the ash trays crammed with butts.

"Go and open the safe," Lola said.

"Not tonight," I said. "It's too late. We'll have to try some other time." She stared fixedly at me.

"You heard what I said. Open the safe!"

"He'll be back in four hours. That doesn't give me time to get away."

She came out from behind the counter and crossed to the wall telephone.

"You either open the safe or I'll call the police. Please yourself."

"You said you would give me twenty-four hours!"

"He won't know you have gone until eight o'clock tomorrow morning. He won't think to look in the safe for maybe a day or so. You have all the time you need. Go and open the safe or I'll call the police!"

I saw she wasn't bluffing. I went back to the garage and collected the bag of tools. The time was ten minutes after ten. I couldn't hope to reach Tropica Springs now before three o'clock in the morning. There would be no train. I would have to ditch the station wagon as soon as I got into town. Jenson had only to telephone the police that I had taken the station wagon for them to descend on me like a swarm of flies. I would now have to hide up in Tropica Springs until the morning. With the hair bleach and a change of clothes, I still stood a good chance.

As I crossed over to the bungalow a truck pulled up by the pumps. I saw Lola come out of the lunch room and go over to the truck.

I went into the sitting-room, turned on the light, pushed aside the settee that hid the safe and squatted down on my heels beside it.

I spun the knob of the dial. It worked smoothly and that was a good sign. Then crouching forward, with my ear pressed against the cold steel of the door, I began to move the dial very gently and slowly from left to right.

In a few seconds I heard the first tumbler drop into place. I reversed the dial and began again. There was nothing to it. You just had to know by experience when the faint sound told you the tumbler had dropped. As a safe, this one was the biggest swindle of them all.

Six times I went through the operation, then I reached out and pulled the door open. It had taken eleven minutes by my strap watch.

The money was there. Neatly stacked in 100-dollar bills: one hundred packets, lovingly put away for the three-year trip around the world.

I reached for the bag, then took hold of the first pack of bills. I heard a sound behind me.

"What in God's name are you doing, Jack?"

Jenson's voice went through me like a sword thrust. For maybe two seconds I remained crouched before the open safe, my hand still on the stack of bills, then slowly I looked over my shoulder.

Jenson stood in the doorway, staring at me. His expression was shocked and bewildered.

I became vaguely aware of the roar of the truck's engine as the truck moved off. I remained crouching before the safe, unable to do anything but stare at Jenson.

He moved his ponderous bulk into the room.

"Jack! What do you think you're doing?"

Slowly I stood up.

"I'm sorry, Mr. Jenson," I said. "It must look to you as if I were going to steal your money, but I wasn't. I give you my word. I know it looks like it, but you've got to believe me."

Then Lola appeared in the doorway. She was white as a fresh fall of snow and she was shaking.

"What's going on here?" she cried, her voice shrill. "Did he open the safe? I knew it! I warned you, Carl! I knew he wasn't

73

to be trusted. He must have sneaked in here while I was in the kitchen!"

Jenson didn't seem to hear her. He was still staring at me.

"What are you doing in here, Jack?" he asked. There was real agony in his voice. It cut into me like the thong of a whip. "Have you got an explanation?"

"Yes. I've got an explanation. First, I'm not Jack Patmore: that's not my name. I'm Chet Carson. I escaped from Farnworth jail six weeks ago."

I saw his heavy face tighten. Moving slowly, he went over to the settee and sat down.

"I read about that. So you're Carson . . ."

"Yes. She saw a photograph of me in an old paper that came in the groceries box on Tuesday. She recognised me. She said if I didn't open the safe so she could steal your money she would give me to the police."

"You liar!" Lola screamed. "Carl! Don't listen to him! He's lying! He's trying to save his rotten skin! I'm going to call the police!"

Jenson turned slowly and stared at her.

"I'll call the police when I want them. You keep out of this."

"He's lying, I tell you! You don't believe him, do you?"

"Will you be quiet!"

She leaned against the wall. Her breasts under the white overall heaved as she tried to steady her breathing.

To me, he said, "What else, Jack? Or isn't there anything else?"

"I planned to take the money," I said. "I was going to clip her on the jaw and take the money to Tropica Springs. I was going to send it back to you with a letter telling you the truth. That way you would believe me and save yourself a lot of grief in the future."

He stared fixedly at me for fully five seconds. I stared right back at him. Then he turned slowly and stared at Lola. She flinched from his probing eyes.

"You say he is lying, Lola?"

"Of course he's lying!"

"Then look at me."

But she couldn't. She tried, but every time her eyes met his, her eyes shifted. She just couldn't take that probing, steady stare.

Slowly he got to his feet. Somehow he seemed now older and his great shoulders sagged.

"Go to bed, Lola. I'll talk about this tomorrow. Never mind the night shift. I'll handle it. Go to bed."

"What's going to happen to him?" she demanded. "I'm going to call the police!"

74

He crossed the room and took her arms in his great hands and gave her a hard little shake.

"Go to bed! No one is calling the police!"

He pushed her out of the room, then he turned and went over to the settee and sat down.

I still stood by the open safe.

"I don't expect you to believe me," I said. "I just couldn't face going back to Farnworth so I was a sucker for her blackmail."

"Funny how these things work out, isn't it?" he said in a low, flat voice. "The President of the Legion had a heart attack just before he left for the meeting. When I got there, the meeting was cancelled. Because a guy has a heart attack, another guy finds out he's married a tramp."

I stiffened.

"You mean you believe me? You don't think I'm lying?"

He looked at me, his hands rubbing his knees.

"I told you: I don't make mistakes about men, Jack, but it seems I do about women."

I drew in a long, deep breath.

"Thanks," I said. "You would have got the money back. There was no other way to save it."

He looked at the open safe and shrugged his shoulders.

"You'll have to go, Jack. You won't be safe here now. She'll give you away. You can be sure of that."

"Yes."

"I'll give you a stake and you can take the station wagon. Any idea where you'll go?"

"New York. I can get lost there."

"I'm going to give you thirty thousand bucks," Jenson said "With that, you'll be able to start up in business."

I gaped at him.

"Oh, no! I couldn't take as much as that, Mr. Jenson. Don't think I'm not grateful, but I just couldn't take it."

"You can and you will," he said, looking directly at me. "I won't be going on this world trip alone. I don't need the money now, and you do. I've never met a guy I like better than you, Jack. You're going to take it." He looked away as he went on, "I'll miss you."

Then I saw her.

She had been pretty quick, for she had changed from her overall to her green dress. Her face was white and her eyes glittered.

In her right hand she held a .45 revolver, and she was pointing it at us.

CHAPTER SEVEN

I

FOR some seconds there was no sound in the room except the ticking of the clock on the overmantel and Lola's quick, sharp breathing.

Jenson was staring at her and at the gun as if he couldn't believe his eyes.

"Why, Lola . . ."

"Don't move!" Her voice was harsh. "I'm taking the money! He's not having a nickel of it!"

"Lola! Have you gone crazy? Put that gun down! It's loaded!"

"Don't move and listen to me. I've had enough of this life. I've had enough of you and your convict pal! I'm going, and I'm taking that money. Don't either of you imagine you can stop me."

Jenson's face hardened.

"You should be ashamed of yourself—talking that way. That money was for both of us. I've slaved thirty-five years to save it and you're not walking off with it now. Put that gun down, and stop acting like a crazy fool!"

"I'm taking it! If you try to stop me I'll tell the police you have been sheltering this jail-bird, and I'll tell them you haven't paid tax on that money! Now get out of my way or you'll be sorry!"

Jenson, his face suddenly red with anger, got to his feet.

I still stood by the open safe. It made me nervous to see the way she was waving the gun about as she talked.

"It's time you were taught a lesson, young woman," Jenson said. "I've been too soft with you. What you want is a good hiding, and that's what you are going to get!"

"Watch it!" I said sharply. I gave the safe door a hard shove with my knee. It swung to with a clang.

Lola, her face tightening with frustrated rage, looked towards me. She knew enough about that safe to realise it had automatically locked as the door slammed shut.

Jenson had almost reached her when the .45 went off with a bang that rattled the windows.

I looked with horror at Jenson.

He stood motionless for a brief moment, then his great body of muscle and flesh collapsed like a felled tree. It went down slowly and ponderously, smashing the back off a chair, sweeping aside the table and shaking the bungalow as it finally hit the floor.

Lola screamed and dropped the gun. She hid her face in her hands, turning her back.

Shaking, I knelt beside Jenson. Blood made a small red patch on his left side. It had been an unlucky shot. The soft-nosed .45 slug had killed him instantly.

I couldn't believe it. I put my hand on his arm, staring at him. The words jerked out of me: "You've killed him!"

She gave a shuddering groan and ran blindly out of the room. I heard her bedroom door slam shut.

I knelt there, staring down at Jenson, not knowing what to do. I didn't dare call the police. Suppose she told them I had killed Jenson? She might do it to save her own skin. She might tell them who I was, and they wouldn't need any further proof once they knew I was the escaped convict from Farnworth.

Then I heard the sudden sound of a car pulling up and the impatient blast from its horn.

The blind in the sitting-room wasn't drawn. Whoever it was outside could see the light. If I didn't get out to them fast they might come over and look in: if they did, they would see Jenson dead on the floor.

As I started for the door, my foot kicked against the .45. I picked it up and shoved it into my hip pocket. I jerked open the front door and started across to the pumps.

There was a big Chrysler waiting: a de luxe job with a customs built body. A blonde woman sat in the front passenger seat. The driver, a thick-set, elderly man, was getting out of the car.

"Fill her up," he said as I reached him, "and how about some food?"

I was in a daze. I scarcely heard what he said. I began automatically to fill the tank.

"Hey! Didn't you hear me?" the man said, raising his voice. "We want something to eat!"

"Sorry—the lunch room's closed."

I wanted to get rid of these two, but the man was one of those wealthy, arrogant big wheels you couldn't brush off.

"Then damn well open it!" he said. "We're hungry. It's your business to provide food."

"I'm sorry, sir, but the lunch room's closed," I said, screwing on the cap of the tank.

"Do you own this joint?"

"No."

77

"Then where's the boss? I'll talk him into opening your god-damn lunch room!"

"Harry, dear . . ." the blonde woman began nervously.

He turned on her.

"You keep out of this! I'll handle it. I'll talk to the top man. I never waste my time talking to hired hands."

To my alarm, he began to walk off towards the bungalow.

"Okay, okay," I said, jumping to his side. "I'll fix you something. The boss is asleep."

He paused to glare at me. "I've a mind to report you."

"I'll fix you something," I said, and leaving him, I opened up the lunch room and turned on the lights.

I heard him bellow at his wife, "Well, come on! Don't sit there! You're hungry, aren't you?"

They followed me into the lunch room and sat down at one of the tables.

"What have you got?" the man barked at me.

"Chicken sandwiches or cold roast beef," I said. The thought of food made me feel sick to my stomach.

"Chicken, and hurry it up. See your hands are clean before you touch the bread."

I went into the kitchen. There was a bottle of Scotch on the table. I picked it up and took a long pull. Then I got the chicken out of the ice box and cut several rounds of sandwiches. I heated coffee, put the food on a tray and carried it into the lunch room.

The man grunted at me, and began to devour the sandwiches. Suddenly I turned cold and my mouth began to fill with bile. It had been a mistake to have drunk that whisky. I felt if I didn't get out into the open air I would faint: I felt that bad.

I mumbled something about fixing his car and I went out fast. The hot night air didn't help me. I just managed to get around to the side of the lunch room before I threw up.

After some minutes I began to recover. I sat on the ground with my back against the wall, my head in my hands, and con-sidered my position.

I was in a jam.

As soon as Lola had got over the shock of her husband's death, and I had an idea it wouldn't take her long, she would realise she was also in a jam.

It hadn't crossed my mind that Jenson's death had been any-thing but an accident. She had been waving the gun around in her fury and it had gone off. But she couldn't prove to the police it had been an accident. They would want to know what she had been doing with a gun in her hand. She would have to admit she was going to steal her husband's savings. Once she admitted that, they would nail her on a murder charge.

How long would it take her to realise her only way out was to fasten Jenson's death on me? I was hand-made for the job.

She could tell the police that she and I had been left together while Jenson had gone to the Legion meeting. She had been busy in the kitchen. I had sneaked into the bungalow and had opened the safe. Jenson had returned unexpectedly and had caught me red-handed. I had killed him. Nothing I could say would shake that kind of evidence once they found out who I was.

My first panicky thought was to get into the station wagon and make a dash for Tropica Springs, but I knew I couldn't beat the speed of a telephone call. As soon as she found I had gone, she would call the police and they would be waiting for me at the bottom of the pass. Even if I disconnected the telephone and tied her up, the chances of someone arriving at the pumps and finding her was too great.

Then suddenly it flashed into my mind that if she had me in a jam, I had her in one too. I realised everything depended on how much she wanted that money in the safe, and I was pretty sure she wanted it more than anything else in the world.

If she gave me away to the police, I had only to tell them that the money in the safe was untaxed and she would never touch it. That had been her threat to Jenson: it could now be mine to her. If I told the police the truth about the money she would never lay her hands on it. This could be stalemate if I handled it right.

I thought of Jenson's body lying in the sitting-room of the bungalow. I would have to bury him. I would also have to think up a story to explain away his absence.

This was as far as I got.

The man and his blonde wife came out of the lunch room and started for their car. I got shakily to my feet and followed them. He paid me the exact amount. He said the place was a disgrace and he would tell his friends about it.

When they had driven away, I ran back to the bungalow.

I was just in time.

As I pushed open the front door, I heard the telephone bell tinkle.

She was calling the police.

II

The telephone was in the hall.

Lola looked up, her finger poised over the dial. She looked ghastly: her face was white, her eyes sunk into her head, and they were scared. Even her lips were white.

We stared at each other. She held the receiver in her hand. I held the .45 in mine, and I pointed it at her.

"Hang up," I said. "Quick!"

The whiteness of her face turned grey as she looked at the gun. I could see she thought I was going to murder her. Shakily she replaced the receiver.

"Go into your bedroom. We've got to talk."

She backed into the room and I followed her, closing the door and leaning against it.

"Were you calling the police?" I asked.

She sank on the bed, her clenched fists between her knees, staring at me.

"Did you imagine it would be an idea to pin his death on me?" I went on. "I'll tell you why it isn't such a hot idea. You'd better not do it if you want the money in the safe. If the police arrest me, I'll tell them your husband never paid tax on the money. They'll love that. By the time the tax boys have slapped on fines, there won't be much left for you—if anything. So if you want that money, watch out."

I saw by her sudden change of expression that what I had said had made an impression.

"I can't keep you away from the telephone if you're determined to use it," I said. "but I'm warning you: give me away to the police and I'll see you don't get that money. It's up to you. The alternative is to bury him, put out a story that he has gone away, and then after a while, when I think it is safe, you can have the money and I'll go off somewhere."

"It was an accident," she said, her voice a husky whisper. "If you hide his body and they find it, they'll say it was murder."

Well, at least, she now seemed ready to discuss the situation. I began to breath more easily.

"Can you prove it was an accident? If you had been alone here when it happened you might possibly get away with it, but not with me here. You'd better make up your mind what you are going to do. If you don't want the money, call the police. I won't stop you. If you want the money, then we'll bury him."

It was a nervy five or six seconds while I waited and while she stared at me, hesitating.

I was pretty sure she wouldn't call the police, but if she had made a move to the telephone I would have stopped her.

She said finally, "Give me the money now. I'll leave here. I promise I won't tell anyone about you."

"No! You'll only get the money when I've decided it is safe for you to have it, and not before. If you can't wait for it, then call the police and lose the lot!"

She realised then the jam she was in. Her disappointment, her frustration and her fury showed clearly on her face.

"Get out of here!" she screamed at me. "Get out!"

She threw herself face down on the bed and began to sob wildly.

I knew then I had won. I went out of the room, shutting the door. I would give her a little time to get over her hysterics, then she would have to help me bury him.

I looked at my watch. The time was just on half-past eleven: too early yet to make a start. I had to be sure when we did bury him we wouldn't be interrupted.

I walked over to the lunch room, and for something to do I cleared up the kitchen. I took my time, trying not to think of anything at all, but every now and then the picture of that great muscular body lying on the sitting-room floor would creep into my mind.

Between eleven-thirty and one a.m. five trucks pulled in for gas. But after one, the traffic ceased and I decided to see how Lola was making out.

The light was still showing through her bedroom blind as I approached the bungalow. I went to her bedroom. Turning the handle, I found the door locked.

"Lola! Come on! You've got to help me!"

"Keep away from me!" she screamed through the panels of the door. "I'm not helping you! You'll never make me do it! Keep away from me!"

She sounded hysterical and half out of her mind. I hadn't time to bother with her in that condition. I would have to do the job on my own.

I had thought about where I was going to bury him. At first I thought I would take him out and bury him in the desert, but there was always a chance someone might come along as I was digging the grave, and finally I decided I would bury him in one of the repair sheds. This particular shed had an earth floor.

I collected a pick-axe and a shovel and went into the shed. I started to dig in a far corner near a pile of scrap metal.

The night was still hot and I hadn't got down more than a foot before sweat was pouring off me. But I kept at it, and finally I got down to four feet, and that was enough. By then the time was half-past three. I climbed out of the hole and went over to my cabin. I took a shower, washing the dirt and sweat off me. Then I put on a pair of clean overalls and walked over to the bungalow.

Lola's bedroom light was still on. As I entered the hall, I paused to listen. I could hear no sound. I pushed open the lounge door, fumbled for the switch and flicked it down.

Jenson's great body lay where it had fallen. He hadn't bled much. There was little blood on the carpet.

I touched him. He was beginning to stiffen. In another hour, and with his weight, I wouldn't be able to handle him. As it was, I was sure I hadn't the strength to get him up on my back and carry him across to the shed. He must have weighed over two hundred and thirty pounds.

I stood looking down at him. It was an odd thing, but I found he was just dead flesh to me. I had got over the shock of his death by now. His personality had gone when he had died. This vast, stiffening body meant nothing to me. Carl Jenson, the man I liked and admired, had departed from it. It was just a threat to me that had to be got rid of as quickly as possible.

I went back to the shed and got a hand truck we used to shift the heavy scrap metal. I trundled it over to the bungalow and bumped it up the steps into the hall. I made a lot of noise, not caring, but Lola didn't come out to see what was going on. She must have guessed, of course, and it irritated me that she was so determined not to help me.

I lugged Jenson's body onto the truck, then I stepped to the front door and looked up and down the long winding road to make sure there were no trucks coming out of the night to surprise me.

I could see no distant headlights. The big yellow moon hung above the mountains like the face of a well-fed mandarin.

I went back into the lounge, caught hold of the handle of the truck and pulled the truck into the hall. As I was manoeuvring it to the front door, the telephone bell began to ring.

The sudden, unexpected shrill note of the bell made my heart do a somersault. I stared at the telephone that stood on a small table in the hall.

I hesitated, then letting go of the truck handle, I went over to the instrument and lifted the receiver.

"Hello?"

Who could be calling at this hour of the morning? By my watch it was now twenty minutes to four.

"Is that you, Jenson?"

The voice was loud and aggressive.

"No. Who's calling?"

"I want Mr. Jenson. Tell him it's Hal Lasch. I want to talk to him."

I looked at Jenson's body as it lay on the truck. Sweat was running down my face and into my eyes.

"Mr. Jenson is asleep," I said. "I can't disturb him."

"You tell him it's Hal Lasch. He'll talk to me. I want his advice on the president's funeral. I want to know if he will do the oration. He won't mind you waking him. You tell him it's Hal Lasch."

"I'll tell him in the morning. He'll call you. I'm not disturbing him now."

"Who the hell are you?" His voice was now a bellow. "You do what I tell you! I know Carl. He'll want to talk to me!"

I drew in a long, deep breath.

"Never mind who I am," I said, matching his own aggressive tone. "You or no other goddamn Swede is disturbing Mr. Jenson at this hour. He's in bed, and his wife is sleeping with him. Do you imagine I'm going in there and wake them because you want to talk about a funeral oration at four o'clock in the morning? You call tomorrow," and I slammed down the receiver.

I stood by the telephone waiting for him to call back, but he didn't. I waited maybe for three minutes—it seemed like three hours, then still sweating and with my nerves sticking a yard out of my skin, I went once more to the front door, checked the empty road, then manhandled the truck out of the bungalow. I trundled it over to the shed and got it alongside the grave I had dug.

I got him into the grave and then shovelled in the soil.

It took me the best part of an hour to get the grave filled in and stamped flat. It was a hell of a way to bury a man as good and as fine as Jenson, but there was nothing I could do better if I were going to save myself from the gas chamber.

I felt I should have said a prayer over him, but I had forgotten any prayers I might have known, I just hoped he would understand and I let it go like that, but I felt bad.

I moved a heavy work bench over the grave, swept up, put the pick-axe and shovel away and then surveyed the scene. I had made a thorough job of it. No one would know nor even guess that a dead man lay four feet below that work bench.

I turned off the light and went across to my cabin. I stripped off and took another shower, then I went to my bed and lay down.

Already the grey light of the dawn was making the mountains sharp etched against the sky. In another hour the sun would be up.

My mind was too restless and uneasy to think of sleep. I lit a cigarette, and stared up at the ceiling.

Now was the time to cook up a story to take care of Jenson's permanent absence. This Swede—Hal Lasch—would be telephoning sometime in the morning. I had to take care of him. I felt sudden panic grip me. If my story wasn't good and wasn't put over convincingly, someone, even if it wasn't Lasch, would become suspicious and the police would move in. They would only have to check on me and I would be cooked. My story had to be good.

By six-thirty, when the first truck to go over the mountain

pulled in for gas, I had a story that satisfied me. It wasn't one hundred per cent foolproof, but at least it was believable.

I rolled off my bed, feeling hot and tired, and I walked over to the pumps.

The trucker nodded to me. He was fat and elderly and his sweaty unshaven face told me he had been driving all night.

"How about some coffee, bud?" he said. "You open yet?"

"Sure. Stick around. I'll fix it for you."

I shot gas into his tank, then went over the lunch room, opened up and heated some coffee.

He came in and sat on a stool, rubbing his eyes and yawning.

I put the cup of coffee in front of him.

"Do you want anything to eat?" I said. "Eggs and ham?"

"Yeah. Eggs and ham is fine."

While I was fixing the meal, he lit a cigarette, and putting his elbows on the counter, he groaned to himself.

"I guess I'll have to quit in a year or so. This racket's getting too tough for a guy my age," he said. "Where's the big Swede? In bed?"

That was what it was going to be now for months: Where's the big Swede? You couldn't have the personality Carl Jenson had and get forgotten.

"He's out of town," I said. "He's gone down to Parker, Arizona. He plans to open another filling station down there."

That was my story and I might as well rehearse it. I saw the trucker look interested.

"Is that right?" He took a drag on his cigarette, letting the smoke drift down his wide nostrils. "That Swede is smart. I've been coming through No Return now for the past fifteen years: regular every two months. I've watched this place grow. Sooner or later, I've said to myself, that Swede is either going to quit or expand. Arizona, huh? That's a hell of a long ways from here."

"I guess so. There's a station already there and it's going for a song. All he has to do is to walk in, and in three months he reckons he'll double the take."

"That's smart." The trucker wagged his head. "What's going to happen here? You looking after it?"

"That's right . . ." I hesitated before I went on, knowing this was the curse. "Me and Mrs. Jenson."

He looked up sharply, frowning.

"Mrs. Jenson is staying on here then?"

"Just for a couple of months until Mr. Jenson can get a good man to take care of the Parker station. I couldn't handle this set-up on my own."

"That's a fact." I could see the surprise and the growing 'Hey-

hey-hey! What's-going-on-around-here?' expression in his eyes.
"Mighty nice looking girl—Mrs. Jenson."

Go on, you big sonofabitch, I thought. Think what you like.
You'll never prove anything.

"Certainly is." I dished up the ham and slid three eggs onto a
plate. I put the plate down in front of him.

I saw he was studying me the way everyone else when they
heard the news would study me.

"So you and she are running this place from now on—that
it?"

"She's running it. I'm just the hired man," I said. "But only
for a couple of months. Mr. Jenson will be back by then."

He grunted and started eating.

I went into the kitchen, leaving the door open, and began load-
ing potatoes into the peeling machine. When I had the machine
working I went over to the deep freeze cabinet and checked on the
food we had in store. Then I sat down and wrote out the lunch
menu, aware this had been Jenson's job; aware now I was taking
his place.

I took the menu card into the lunch room and hung it up. The
trucker had finished his meal. He paid me.

We went out together to his truck, talking. As he was climbing
into the cab, I saw Lola come out of the bungalow.

She was wearing a pair of scarlet shorts and a white halter. In
that rig-out her shape was sensational.

The trucker paused and sucked in his breath sharply while he
stared at her, then he looked at me and grinned.

"I wouldn't mind being in your place, pal. Strikes me you have
a pretty sweet job."

He slammed the cab door shut, winked at me, gunned his
engine and drove off. As he passed Lola, he gave a shrill wolf
whistle.

CHAPTER EIGHT

I

I FOUND Lola in the kitchen. As I came in, she turned and faced me. She looked pretty bad. There were circles around her eyes, her face was pale and drawn and I guessed, like me, she hadn't had much sleep.

I was furious that she had been so stupid and thoughtless to have put on the get-up she wore.

"Do you have to show your body off like this?" I snarled at her. "Do you want every goddamn tongue to start wagging about us?"

She looked blankly at me.

"What do you mean?"

"Use your head!" I reached for her overall and threw it at her. "That trucker saw you just now. He said I had a sweet job. He knows we're alone together. That's the way talk starts. Before we know it, we'll have the police here!"

Sulkily, she put on the overall.

"What have you done with him?" she asked, not looking at me.

"I've buried him. Now listen, we're going to run this place together," I said. "I won't interfere with you and you're not going to interfere with me. When I think it's okay to move, I'll go, and when I go I'll open the safe and you'll get the money."

She looked sharply at me, her eyes glittering.

"When will that be?"

"I don't know. I'm not moving from here until I'm satisfied the hunt for me is over. You'll have to make up your mind to wait."

Her mouth became sulky again.

"Carl has friends. They'll want to know where he is."

"Do you think I haven't got that worked out?" I said, impatiently. "You will tell them he has gone to Arizona to investigate another filling station. We don't expect him back for a couple of months. In the meantime you are running this place and I'm helping you."

"And then? What happens? They won't forget him. They'll keep asking."

"At the end of a couple of months you will get a letter from him. He'll tell you he has found another woman he likes better than you and he is not coming back. That kind of bad news is believed because people want to believe it. Because he feels he has treated you badly, he is giving Point of No Return to you. You will continue to run it with me until I'm sure it is safe to quit, then when I've gone, you can get rid of it if you want to."

"I have a better idea," she said, resting her hips against the kitchen table. "Open the safe now and you can have the thirty thousand dollars Carl was going to give you. With that money you can get away."

"No! I wouldn't touch his money. I'm safe here and I'm staying here! When I'm ready, you'll have the money, but not before."

Two little spots of red showed in her cheeks and she started to say something but stopped as we heard the sound of a car pulling up.

Leaving her, I went out into the lunch room as the screen door pushed open. A heavily-built man, tall and beefy, with sandy hair, prominent blue eyes and around forty, came in.

He gave me a long hard stare before saying, "Where's Jenson?"

I had an idea who he was. Obviously he was a Swede and besides, I recognised his aggressive voice.

"He's out," I said. "Anything I can do?"

"Out? At this hour? Where's he gone?"

"Anything I can do?" I repeated, "or do you want to talk to Mrs. Jenson?"

Hearing voices, Lola came to the kitchen door. As soon as she saw the big Swede, the sulky look went away and she smiled at him.

"Why, hello, Mr. Lasch, you're early."

He relaxed a little and tipped his hat.

"Morning, Mrs. Jenson. I came over to talk to Carl about Wallace's funeral. I guess Carl told you the poor guy had a heart attack last night. The Legion want to do the right thing by him. As Carl was an old friend and an important member of the Legion, we thought maybe he would do the oration. This fella tells me Carl isn't here."

I looked at Lola. She was quite calm. At the mention of Wallace's death, her smile faded and she looked sorrowful. She was certainly some actress.

"That's right. You've just missed him. He left for Tropica Springs about half an hour ago."

Lasch gaped at her.

"Carl did? His car's in the shed. I saw it as I came in."

My heart began to pound, but I needn't have worried. She was a fluent liar, and she was more than capable of handling a big, dumb Swede like Lasch.

"He didn't take the car. He'll be away for a few weeks. He got a lift into Tropica Springs on a truck. I couldn't be left here without the car for so long. He'll be sorry to have missed you."

I could see Lasch was surprised and puzzled by all this. He lifted his hat to scratch his head, then he said, "You mean he won't be back in time for the funeral, Mrs. Jenson?"

"Oh no. I don't really know quite when he will be back. Several weeks . . . He had the chance last night to buy another filling station. He had just got back after the meeting had been cancelled. Someone called and made him this offer. We talked it over. He decided to go down there and take a look."

Lasch squinted at her. "Down where?"

"Some place in Arizona," Lola said. "He has always wanted to own another filling station. This sounded like a bargain so he rushed off before it is snapped up."

I couldn't have done better myself. She really could tell the tale.

"Arizona? Why, that's miles away," Lasch said blankly. "He isn't planning to leave here for good, is he?"

"We haven't got around to that yet. I think his idea is to put someone in charge down there. I'm sure he'll tell you about it, Mr. Lasch, when he comes back."

That pulled him up short. He looked a little embarrassed.

"I didn't mean to sound inquisitive. I'm surprised not to find him here. Well, if he won't be back for some weeks I guess I'll have to deliver the oration myself." He looked at me. "Who's this fella?"

"Jack Patmore," Lola said. "He's helping out while Carl is away."

Lasch looked me over, his eyes hostile.

"Are you the guy who called me a goddamn Swede last night on the telephone?"

I matched his look.

"At four o'clock in the morning I'm likely to call anyone anything."

He hesitated, grunted, then turned his back on me.

Lola said, "Won't you have breakfast, Mr. Lasch? It's all ready."

"No, thanks. I've a lot to do. When Carl gets back, ask him to call me, will you?"

She said she would and he left without looking at me.

There was a pause, then Lola went back into the kitchen.

Well, at least, the story was accepted. There would be talk of course about Lola and me out here alone together. I remembered what Carl had told me, how when she first came here to work for him the talk got so bad he married her to shut their mouths.

This day was Sunday. On Sundays we had a lot of traffic over the mountain, and we were both kept busy. We served thirty lunches and twenty-three dinners. I had a major repair job, to say nothing of serving gallons of gas.

By the time the traffic slacked off, it was close on midnight.

During the day Lola hadn't said a word to me. Now when I walked into the kitchen just as she was finishing clearing up, she didn't look round nor show she knew I was there.

"Pretty good day," I said, leaning against the door post. "I reckon we've taken close on four hundred bucks."

She put the pan she had been scouring on the shelf. I might not have spoken for all the notice she took of me. She took off her soiled overall, rolled it and tossed it into the laundry basket.

I felt a stab of desire go through me to see her again in those halter and shorts. It was a physical urge and made me go hot. I had to fight down the impulse to cross the room and grab her.

She went out by the back door, leaving me alone in the kitchen.

I turned off the lights and locked up.

So she was going to sulk, I thought as I walked over to my cabin. Well, okay, we'll see who gets tired of that first. I went into my bedroom, crossed over to the window to pull down the blind, then paused.

The light was on in her bedroom. She hadn't pulled down the blind. I could see into the room. She was standing directly under the light. She had taken off her halter and as I watched she stepped out of her shorts.

I stood there, watching her, my heart bumping unevenly against my ribs. I watched her, naked as the back of my hand, turn and walk to the bathroom, enter and close the door.

I had to make a conscious effort to reach out and pull down the blind.

II

The next four days followed the same pattern.

Lola didn't speak to me. It was as if I wasn't there. She ran the kitchen entirely on her own, and she kept the kitchen door locked. We had a service hatch at the back of the lunch counter. I called the orders through this and I only caught an occasional glimpse of her when I peered through the opening at her. I did all the waiting, the servicing of the cars, and I ran the lunch room snack bar single handed.

The nights also followed the same pattern. She did no night duty, leaving it to me. Around eleven o'clock she would unlock the kitchen door and go out the back way to the bungalow, leaving me to manage as best I could.

She didn't lower her blind when she went to bed, but although the temptation was great, I kept away from my cabin until her light went out.

The picture I had in my mind of her nakedness remained to torture me. The heat didn't help either. After the fourth day, a strong wind got up, blowing sand everywhere, a hot wind that frayed my nerves.

I began to sleep badly.

The heat got so bad the traffic dropped off. The Cantaloup growers began to send their produce by train as the eighteen hour run from Oakland over the mountain to Tropica Springs spoilt the fruit. Fewer tourists used the blistering, sun scorched road. Receipts dropped off. There were less meals to serve and no repairs. I found I had time on my hands, and as my mind was constantly tormented by the thoughts of Lola, this was a pretty bad period for me.

Eight days after Jenson's death, Lola made her first trip to Wentworth for provisions.

I was working on the magneto of the Station wagon for something to do when I heard the Mercury start up. Looking out, I saw her driving away. I guessed where she was going. It irritated me that she had gone, not telling me when she would be back, not caring that I would have to handle whatever trade came in single handed.

Around eleven o'clock, and as I was reassembling the magneto, I heard a car draw up. I was in the middle of fixing the timing and I cursed under my breath. I couldn't leave what I was doing, so I carried on, letting the driver wait.

Three minutes or so later, I had got it fixed, and I straightened up, reaching for a rap to wipe off my hands when I saw the shadow of a man lying across the opening of the shed. I looked up. My heart contracted as I saw George Ricks standing there, in his dirty overalls, his straw hat resting at the back of his head. His dog stood behind him, staring mournfully at me.

I had completely forgotten Ricks. Here was danger. The sight of this tall, stooping vulture of a man sent a chill crawling up my spine.

"Mornin'," he said, squinting at me. "Where's Carl?"

I picked up the rag and began to wipe my sweating hands with it.

"Mr. Jenson is away. What do you want?"

"Away?" He moved a few steps into the shed. The dog moved with him, keeping close to his right leg. "What do you mean—away?"

90

"What do you want?"

"Look, young fella, it's my business what I want and not yours. You're the hired hand, aren't you, or do you suddenly own this place?"

"I don't own it. I'm asking you—what do you want?"

"Where's that Jezebel? Isn't she here?"

"I don't know what you mean. What Jezebel?"

He leered at me.

"His wife. Who do you think you are kidding? Where is she?"

"If it's any business of yours—she's in Wentworth."

"So you're in charge?"

"Someone has to be."

He leaned forward and scratched the dog's head. The dog flinched as if expecting a blow.

"Where's Mr. Jenson gone?"

"He's away on business."

He gave the dog a sudden impatient shove with his leg as he asked, "What business?"

"You'd better ask him."

He eyed me, moving a few steps forward.

"When will he be back?"

"I don't know: a couple of months: maybe not so long."

"A couple of months?" His mean face showed his surprise. "What's going on around here? Didn't he take his wife with him?"

"Look, I'm busy," I said curtly. "Mr. Jenson won't be back for a couple of months. What do you want?"

"I want to see him. It's important. Where is he?"

"Somewhere in Arizona. He's buying a filling station if you must know."

"Is that right?" He put his head on one side, squinting at me. "Another filling station? I guess he has more money than sense. You mean he didn't take his wife with him?"

"No."

"She's staying here while he's away?"

"Yes."

I could see his dirty mind was already buzzing like a beehive.

"Well, I'll be darned! I always thought he was an old fool, but I didn't imagine he would be that much of a fool."

"Who cares what you think?"

He stared at me, then his crafty, mean face lit up with a sly grin.

"Well, I can't call you a fool. You seem to know a good thing when you find it, don't you?"

"Mr. Jenson told me about you," I said, and I didn't bother to conceal my contempt for him. "He said you were the biggest scrounger in the district. He said if you ever came around here trying to take something, I was to throw you out. Are you getting out or do I throw you out?"

"Is that what he said?" The sly grin slipped a little. "He said that about his own brother-in-law? You take it easy, young fella. If Carl is fool enough to leave you and that wife of his alone together, it's no skin off my nose. More fool he: that's what I say. I've got to see him. What's his address?"

"I don't know."

He took off his straw hat and scratched his dirty, scaly scalp while his little eyes probed my face.

"I've got to talk to him. I want his signature on my pension papers. He always signs them. You must know where he is."

"I don't know! He's somewhere in Arizona. He's moving around. He said not to expect to hear from him until he got back."

He gave the dog a sudden flick with his hat before putting the hat back on his head. There was now an alert, suspicious expression on his face.

"*She* must know how to get hold of him."

"I tell you neither of us do!"

"Then what am I going to do about my pension papers? If I don't get them signed, I don't get my pension."

"Get someone else to sign them."

He shook his head.

"I can't do that. Carl always does it. If I get someone else to do it, those dopes will want to know why. They could hold up my pension: then what would I have to live on?"

"I can't help that," I said. "I haven't his address. If I had, I'd give it to you. You'll have to wait until he gets back."

He continued to stare at me, his head on one side. The dog stared at me too.

"Two months you say? What am I going to live on for two months while I'm waiting?"

"I don't know and I don't care!" I found I was shouting at him and I throttled my voice back. "Why don't you do some work for a change?"

He didn't like that. His face turned mean.

"Don't talk that way to me, young fella. I'm a sick man. My doctor won't let me work. I have a bad heart. Are you sure she doesn't know where he is?"

"How many more times do I have to tell you—neither of us do!"

There was a pause while he bent to pat his cringing dog. Then he said, "Suppose something happened? Suppose she got ill? Suppose the place burned down? You'd have to tell him, wouldn't you? How would you find him in an emergency?"

"She's not going to get ill and this place isn't going to burn down! Now, get out! I've things to do."

"If I don't get my pension papers signed I'll have no money." His voice had changed into a whine.

I was tempted to give him a few dollars to get rid of him, but I realised the danger of this. Once I began handing this scrounging rat money, he would keep pestering me.

"Oh, get the hell out of here!" I shouted. "I'm busy!"

I went back to the Station wagon and began to tighten the bolts on the magneto.

"When will she be back?" he asked.

"I don't know—late."

There was a pause, then he said, the whine still in his voice, "How about lending me twenty dollars?"

"It's not my money to lend—beat it!"

I was now working on the magneto, my back turned to him. I was putting pressure on a nut when he said, "I guess if I wrote to the Arizona police they'd find him fast enough."

He had spoken casually, but to me it was like taking a punch under the heart. The spanner slipped and I lost the skin off a knuckle.

I tried to assure myself that the State police wouldn't do a thing about such an inquiry, but there was the risk that they might. If Ricks made enough of it, created suspicion, they might just possibly get in touch with the Wentworth police, and some smart, inquiring cop might come out here and start asking questions. He might even be smart enough to recognise me.

"Mr. Jenson would like it fine to have the police looking for him," I said, trying to make my voice sound casual. I sucked my damaged knuckle. "You be careful what you do. He'd be so mad he'd never sign your goddamn papers."

"Well, I've got to find him!" His voice was now aggressive. "If you can't tell me where he is, the cops might. You talk to her. I wouldn't be surprised if he hadn't told her where he could be found and she isn't telling you. I'll come out tomorrow. You tell her that. If she doesn't know, I'm going to write to the Arizona police."

By now I had my face under control and I turned.

"Okay, okay, I'll talk to her. I'm pretty sure she doesn't know, but I'll ask her."

This was making a concession, and to a man like Ricks, it was a sign of weakness, but the idea of some nosy cop coming out here scared the life out of me.

He nodded: the sly grin once more in place.

"You tell her I'll be out tomorrow evening. Well, I'll run along. That reminds me. I'm nearly out of gas. I may as well fill up while I'm here. I'll have to owe it to you. Carl wouldn't mind."

My one thought was to get rid of him. I shouldn't have let him have the gas, but I was sure if I didn't, he would stay whining until he got it.

"Oh, help yourself, but let me get on with my work!"

"That's a good fella." He grinned widely. "You tell her I've got to get those papers signed. I'll be out here tomorrow evening, around supper time."

He shambled off, followed by his dog, back to his car. I watched him fill the tank and then a couple of five gallon cans. He was one of those mean scroungers who grabbed a yard when you gave him an inch. He got in the car and drove off.

When he was out of sight, I went over to the lunch room. I felt in need of a drink. I poured a big shot of Scotch and drank it, then lighting a cigarette, I paced up and down, trying to assess the danger from this old vulture.

Would the Arizona police take action if he wrote to them? It depended on what he said. If he pointed out that Jenson had disappeared, and his wife and the hired hand were sleeping together, the police might react. Often enough I had read in the newspapers that murders had been discovered by neighbours passing on gossip and rumours to the police. If the police did make enquiries and couldn't find any trace of Jenson coming out of Arizona—his description was an easy one to remember—they might alert the Wentworth police who were never over-worked, and they could come out here. They would want to know who I was and where I had come from.

But how to shut Ricks's mouth? The obvious way would be to give him money. That would hold him for a couple of months. Would he believe my story that at the end of this time, Jenson had found some other woman and had given Point of No Return to Lola? Unless we could show him a letter, telling him it had come from Jenson, he would most certainly not believe such a story. Had he ever seen Jenson's handwriting? I thought it was more than likely. He most certainly knew his signature. It would be too dangerous to attempt to forge the letter.

The more I thought about it, the trickier the situation became. When dealing with a man of Ricks's character, a man with nothing to do and with a flair for smelling out trouble, I would have to watch every move I made.

Finally, when the lunch trade started, I had to give up trying to solve the problem. I had to talk to Lola. We had a common enemy now. Maybe between the two of us, we could think of a way to stall Ricks.

Lola didn't get back until after ten o'clock. By that time, I was pretty worked up, and I had found no solution how to deal with Ricks.

I had just finished clearing up the kitchen and stacking the dishes when I heard the sound of an approaching car. I looked out of the window and saw Lola driving the Mercury into the garage.

I went out and caught up with her as she was crossing over to the bungalow.

"I want to talk to you," I said.

She quickened her step, ignoring me. I walked with her up the path, waited until she had unlocked the front door of the bungalow, then I crowded in with her.

She turned, her green eyes pools of fury.

"Get out!"

"We've got to talk," I said. "Your pal George Ricks was here this morning."

That gave her a jolt. She stiffened. Wariness took the place of anger in her eyes.

"I'm not interested. Get out!"

"You will be."

I crossed the hall and entered the sitting-room. I noticed she had washed out the blood stain in the carpet. I went over to an armchair and sat down.

She stood in the doorway, waiting. She had taken off her hat. Her red hair went well with the green dress. She looked pretty good.

"He wanted your husband to sign his pension papers," I said. "He's going to make trouble. He wanted to know where he could find Jenson."

She didn't say anything. Her face remained expressionless.

"I told him he was somewhere in Arizona. He said he had to get his papers signed or he wouldn't get the pension. When I told him he would have to wait, he said he would write to the Arizona police and ask them to find him."

That jolted her out of her sulky indifference. She moved into the room, shutting the door behind her. She walked over to a chair and sat down. The skirt of her green dress rode up over her knees. She didn't attempt to pull it down. I didn't even look twice. I had too much on my mind to bother about a pair of pretty knees.

"So . . ." She drew in a deep breath. "So much for your bright idea. Well, you'd better start thinking up another idea, hadn't you?"

"Let's quit fighting," I said. "Ricks could make a lot of trouble for both of us. He's coming here tomorrow night to talk to you. Between then and now we'll have to decide what we should do about him. So stop fighting me and start thinking. We're in this jam together, even if you don't think so now. If the police come here, I'll be in trouble and I'll take care you'll be in trouble too. How are we going to keep Ricks quiet?"

She reached for a cigarette and lit it. She let the smoke drift down her nostrils.

"Why worry about him? Open the safe, take your share and get out. I'll go too. When he comes here again, we'll have gone."

"Is that the best you can do?" I said impatiently. "You've got that money on the brain! How can we walk out and leave this place deserted? Talk sense! Imagine someone coming here for gas and finding the place locked and empty. Imagine Ricks coming here. He would tell the police and there would be an investigation."

"We could sell the place."

"Could we? Is it yours to sell?"

She frowned at me. "What do you mean?"

"The only way you could sell it is to prove Jenson is dead and he has willed it to you. How are you going to prove he is dead without the police finding out he was murdered?"

"He wasn't murdered! It was an accident!"

"You tell that to the police and see what happens!"

Her hands turned into fists. I could see by her expression that at last it was dawning on her the kind of trap we were in.

"Give me my share of the money and I'll go," she said. "You can stay here. What's the matter with that? You can say I've gone to join Carl in Arizona, leaving you here to run the place."

"Do you imagine Ricks would believe that? First, Jenson disappears: then you, and I have the place. He'd tell the police I had murdered you both to get it. They might not believe him, but they would come out here and investigate. They would find out who I was. They might even find where I buried Jenson."

That really jolted her.

"You aren't telling me you have been mad enough to bury him *here*?"

"Where else do you imagine I have buried him? You didn't help me, did you? How could I have got him in the Station wagon? He weighed over two hundred pounds. I buried him in the repair shed, and if they suspect I have murdered you two, they'll start digging. If there's one thing they are good at—it's digging. They could find him."

She ran her fingers through her thick hair with a movement of exasperation.

"What are you trying to tell me?" she demanded, her voice shrill. "That we have to stay here *forever*?"

"We have to stay here. I don't know for how long. If we leave now, we're sunk. They'll dig the whole place up and they'll find him, and then they'll come after us. Our one hope is to stay here and make my story stick that he had gone off with another woman."

"I'm not staying!" She pounded her fist on the arm of the chair. "I've had enough of it! I want that money! I'm going to have it!"

I waved my hand towards the safe.

"Go ahead and help yourself," I said and got to my feet. "The money's there if you can open the safe. Maybe when you have thought more about it, you'll see I'm talking sense. You think about it."

I walked out of the bungalow, leaving her, white-faced, her eyes pools of fear and rage.

From then on until midnight, I sat by the pumps, waiting for trade. The hot wind blew around me, stirring the dust and the sand, making my body feel gritty and uncomfortable.

As I sat, staring into the darkness, my mind probed at the problem without getting anywhere. At least, now I didn't feel entirely alone. The lights in the bungalow remained on. I was sweating it out, but she was too.

At half past midnight, I decided to go to my cabin and try to sleep. No truck nor car had come through during the past two hours. There seemed no point in sitting there in the hot wind waiting any longer. As I started towards my cabin, the light in the lounge of the bungalow went out and the light in her bedroom went up. She too, had the same idea.

I took a shower. It helped a little, but not much. I lay on the bed. I saw her light go out. I tried to shut my problem out of my mind and go to sleep but it was useless.

The sound of my bedroom door opening jerked my mind out of its panicky thinking.

I half sat up, staring towards the door lit by the moonlight coming through the window.

A shadowy figure moved into the room. It was Lola. She paused in a puddle of moonlight that lay on the floor. She had on a green silk wrap which she held tightly round her.

We stared at each other, then she came to the bed and sat by my side.

"If we have to stay here together," she said, her voice an intimate whisper, "there's no need for us to remain enemies, is there?"

She leaned over me, her mouth seeking mine . . .

7

CHAPTER NINE

I

A BAND of sunlight coming through the chink in the blind woke me. I stretched, yawning, then lifting my head, I looked at the bedside clock. The time was twenty minutes past six. Lola had gone. It took me a few minutes to realise that she had spent the night with me.

There's no need for us to be enemies she had said, but she hadn't fooled me and she wasn't going to fool me. I was sure all she thought about and all she planned for was to persuade me to open the safe. She was now attempting to break down my resistance by this new intimacy, hoping she would be able to influence me to change my mind and open the safe.

This was going to be a one-sided bargain. The safe was going to remain closed.

I slid off the bed, shaved, showered and dressed. I was curious to see what her attitude was going to be towards me this morning.

I went to the lunch room. The screen door stood open, and there was an appetising smell of ham grilling coming from the kitchen.

I walked around the counter and tentatively pushed at the kitchen door, half expecting to find it locked, but it swung open.

I walked in.

Lola, wearing her neat white overall, was breaking an egg into the fry pan. She looked over her shoulder at me. "Hello, I was beginning to wonder if you were going to sleep all day," she said.

I came up behind her and slid my arms around her, pulling her against me. I kissed the side of her neck.

"Hey! hey! Your eggs will be spoiled," but she leaned against me, her face against mine.

"Are they for me?"

"Who else do you imagine they're for?" She twisted out of my grip and faced me. Then she smiled. "Hello, lover! Any regrets?"

"No regrets."

"Surprised?"

"Knocked for a loop."

She came up to me and slid her arms around my neck, her green eyes glittering. Kissing her was an experience. Her body pressed hard against mine, her fingers moved through my hair.

"Who's spoiling the eggs now?" I said.

She moved away. "Come on and eat then."

I watched her dish up the eggs and slide the ham onto a plate.

"Pour the coffee," she said, putting the plate on the table.

We sat opposite each other. She took a cigarette from the pack and lit it.

"I guess I've been pretty mean to you ever since you came," she said, staring at me. "But I have had a change of heart. I realised we couldn't go on living the way we have been living. Besides, you're attractive and it's been a long time since I've lived near an attractive man. Do you want to move into the bungalow?"

I hesitated for a moment, but only for a moment. In that moment a picture of Jenson came into my mind but I pushed it out fast as I looked at her.

"Yes," I said. "You're attractive too, you know."

She smiled. "I'm not so lousy. Are you going to forget how mean I've been to you?"

"Yes. The moment I saw you, I wanted you."

A truck pulled up by the pumps and the driver sounded his horn.

"I'll fix it," she said. "You finish your breakfast."

As she went past me, she touched my shoulder in that intimate way women in love have, then she went out to the waiting truck.

I finished my breakfast, my mind busy.

I told myself I had to watch out. This is an act, I said to myself, so watch it, but already I was beginning to wish it wasn't an act.

I was running hot water over my breakfast plate when she came back into the kitchen.

"I'll do it," she said.

"It's done." I put the plate in the rack and turned to face her. She moved close to me. I put my hands on her hips, feeling hard flesh alive under my fingers. "Any ideas about Ricks yet? He'll be out here tonight."

"He doesn't worry me. I'll give him some money: ten dollars will be enough. He won't make trouble if he gets some money and we can afford it."

"Don't be too sure. He's dangerous. Once you start giving him money, he'll keep coming back for more."

She shook her head.

"I've handled him before. I can handle him now. You leave him to me."

"Just watch out. He could make trouble."

"I'll watch out."

The hot wind now had died out. It was cooler. By ten o'clock, more traffic was coming through from Oakland. For the rest of the day we were both kept busy.

I found myself enjoying working with Lola. Whenever I went into the kitchen to load up a tray for a waiting customer, we fooled around together, kissing and fondling each other. I enjoyed it a lot, and maybe she did, but I still wasn't that far gone not to be pretty sure this change of heart, as she called it, was an act.

Around seven o'clock, the traffic suddenly fell away and there was a respite. I went into the kitchen and stood around, watching Lola prepare a dozen or so veal cutlets for the evening's menu.

"Instead of devouring me with your eyes, how about peeling some potatoes?" she said.

"Who cares about potatoes?"

I slid my arms around her.

She tried to break free, but I held her. We were wrestling the way lovers do, when I heard the kitchen door creak open. I let go of her and moved away from her fast, but not fast enough.

We both looked towards the kitchen door.

Ricks was standing in the doorway, watching us. There was that sly, poisonous grin on his thin face that told me he had seen what had been going on.

I cursed myself for being such a careless fool for I had known he was coming out this evening.

I looked at Lola.

She was completely unperturbed: her face was expressionless; her eyebrows slightly raised.

I knew I was the give away. I wasn't able to control the guilt nor the fear that was showing on my face.

"I didn't mean to butt in," Ricks said and showed his yellow teeth in a sneering smile. "I said I'd call—remember?"

I just stood there, scared and sweating. No words came.

"Hello, George," Lola said indifferently. "What do you want?"

The small, sly eyes shifted from her to me and from me to her.

"Didn't this fella tell you I'd be looking in? Have you heard from Carl yet?"

She shook her head, still completely unperturbed.

"I don't expect to hear from him until he gets back. He's pretty busy."

"Did this fella tell you about my pension papers?"

"What about them?"

"I want Carl to sign them."

"Any lawyer or bank manager will sign them for you."

He squinted at her, scowling.

"That's where you are wrong. If I go to anyone but Carl my pension could get held up. Then what would I have to live on? Carl's always done it for me."

Lola shrugged indifferently.

"I don't know where he is. He's moving around. You'll have to wait."

Ricks shifted from one foot to the other. I could see he wasn't at ease with Lola. Her steady, indifferent stare seemed to confuse him.

"Maybe I'd better write to the Arizona police," he said. "My pension papers are important."

He was watching her closely, but he didn't get any change out of her.

"Perhaps the police won't think so," she said. "Please yourself. I couldn't care less who you write to. Carl may not be in Arizona for all I know. He said he was going on to Colorado before making up his mind." She leaned her hips against the table and began fiddling with her hair the way women do. With her arms up, her breasts lifted and she looked provocatively sensual. "Don't fuss, George, for heaven's sake. Take your papers to a bank. If you're that hard up, I can lend you something."

It was casually and beautifully done. I wished she had handled him from the start. I saw now that in my clumsy way I had only succeeded in arousing his suspicions. Her approach left him in two minds.

"How much?" He looked eagerly at her. "How much would you lend me?"

"Don't get so worked up," she said, her tone contemptuous. "I'll let you have ten dollars."

His face fell.

"That wouldn't help much. I've got expenses like everyone else. How about twenty dollars?"

"Always the big mouth, George," she said. "You never miss out on a chance, do you?" She walked past him into the lunch room and I heard her open the cash register. The ping of the bell as the drawer slid open made him point like a gun dog.

She came back with three five dollar bills in her hand.

"Here . . ." She thrust the bills at him. "That's all you're getting so don't come here scrounging any more. Carl doesn't want you here, and you know it."

He grabbed the money, putting it hurriedly into his hip pocket.

"You're a hard woman, Lola," he said. "I'm mighty thankful I'm not your husband. I reckon Carl will regret taking you as a wife before long."

"Who cares what you think?" she said and laughed scornfully. "Go away and don't come back pestering me."

COME EASY — GO EASY

"Two's company and three's a crowd, huh?" He looked from her to me. "You two watch out. Carl won't like what's going on around here."

Lola looked at me.

"Kick the scrounger out. I've had enough of him."

As I started towards Ricks, he turned and bolted out of the kitchen. Neither of us moved until we heard his car drive away, then with a grimace, Lola went back to trimming the cutlets.

"He saw us," I said.

"Who cares? I told you I could handle him."

"He'll be back for more money."

She began placing the cutlets on a dish.

"Oh, quit worrying. I can handle him."

II

Two weeks went by and we saw nothing of Ricks. We were busy all the time. A number of people asked for Jenson, but they all accepted the story that he was fixing up another filling station in Arizona. Two or three of them did give Lola and me curious stares, and I could see they were wondering what we were up to alone together. This didn't worry Lola, but it certainly worried me.

We now had a set routine. We both kept the lunch room and the pumps running until one o'clock, then we locked up and spent the rest of the night together in the bungalow.

I didn't like the idea of sharing Jenson's bed with her, but physically, she was so exciting I couldn't resist her. There were times, as we lay exhausted from our violent love-making, when I thought of Jenson in that hastily dug grave, and cold sweat would break out on my body. No such qualms of conscience ever assailed Lola. Jenson was dead. To her, he had never existed.

During those two weeks, it gradually dawned on me that I was falling in love with her. Maybe this was inevitable the way we were living together. From the moment I had first seen her, she had attracted me. Now that we had blunted the edge of our desires, I found myself settling down to a husband-and-wife association with her. This was something that grew during the days I spent with her, and with its growth, my suspicions of her began to fade.

Every now and then it came into my mind that I was playing into her hands, and I would jerk myself alert, but she didn't mention the money nor suggest that I should open the safe, and I soon slipped back into the comfort and the excitement she offered me.

Finally, I began to believe that my love for her was influencing her, and she was as much in love with me as I was with her. I even began to hope that we could remain here together, run the place as Jenson and she had run it, and forget the past.

The time I liked best with her was the half hour before we got up. We would lie side by side in the big bed, watching the sun climb above the mountains while we discussed the day's work, the day's menu and what provisions we would need.

One morning as we lay side by side in the bed, she said suddenly, "Don't you think we should get someone to help out here, Chet? It would be fun to have a night off now and then, wouldn't it? Do you like dancing? We could go to Wentworth and dance. Let's get someone."

I stretched lazily. The idea was tempting, but I knew it would be too dangerous.

"We can't do it, Lola, not yet. If we went together to Wentworth, the gossips would start. Besides, we couldn't have anyone here, living the way we are living. We must wait a couple of months, then after we have put out the story he isn't coming back, we can do something about it, but not before."

She slid one long, bare leg out of bed.

"I'm getting terribly tired of being chained to this place."

"Hang on a little longer. We'll fix something."

She got out of bed.

I watched her cross the room for her wrap. This moment always gave me pleasure to see her, naked, moving across the room, showing off her beautiful body with that liquid grace most Italians have: heavy, sensual, and provocative.

"All right. I'll wait." She put on the wrap. "Will you do the marketing for me this morning? I have a batch of pies to make. I can't spare the time to go into Wentworth, but there's a lot we want. I can look after the pumps while the pies are baking.

I very nearly fell for it, then into my mind came a sudden suspicion. Was this an excuse to get me out of the way? It wouldn't be impossible for her to get a safe man from Tropica Springs to come over and open the safe. She could be gone with the money by the time I got back from Wentworth.

I looked at her.

She was combing her hair, humming under her breath. She was relaxed, but I knew that meant nothing after seeing the way she had handled Ricks.

"I don't think I'd better go, Lola," I said, trying to make my voice sound casual. "The less I'm seen in Wentworth the safer it is for me. Can't you start the pies and leave me to look after them?"

I watched for a change of expression, my heart thumping. I watched for some hint to confirm my suspicions.

She put the comb down, shrugging.

"All right, if you swear you will look after them," she said and came and stood at the foot of the bed, looking questioningly at me. "You really think it isn't safe for you to be seen in Wentworth?"

"I'm not taking any chances."

"You're right. I wouldn't have anything happen to you."

"That's nice to know."

"I mean that, Chet." She smiled at me, and then she said, "I love you."

I slid out of bed and grabbed her.

"I've been waiting for you to say that," I said. "I'm crazy about you too."

She held me tightly.

"I'm happy with you, Chet. I never thought I would be happy with any man, but I'm so tired of this place. There's nothing to do except work: nowhere to go. I'm sick to death of it."

"Stick it a little longer, then we'll go somewhere else. I want to get away too, but we just can't walk out and leave the place and it's too early to attempt to sell it."

"Well, all right." She moved away from me. "I'd better start those pies."

While I was dressing, I thought about what she had said about loving me. I was feeling right on top of the world. I was sure I could trust her.

I went over to the lunch room and got the coffee ready while she fixed the pies.

"Chet . . ."

She turned to look directly at me.

"What do you plan to do? I don't mean now, but in the future. Have you thought about it?"

"I've thought about it. How would you like to marry me for a start?"

She smiled at me.

"I'd like that, but wouldn't we have to prove he was dead?"

"We can't do that. We'll have to think of a way to get away from here without running into trouble. I keep thinking, but it foxes me. Once we do get away from here, we can get lost. We could marry then. How would you like to run a place like this, say in Florida?"

"I wouldn't mind. You mean we'd use the money in the safe to start a business for us both?"

This was the first time she had mentioned the money in the safe. It was casually said, and I looked sharply at her, but she was looking straight back at me and she met my eyes without flinching.

"That would be the idea."

"With all that money we could have a wonderful place, couldn't we, Chet?" Her eyes lit up. "Let's do it soon."

"We have to find a way to get rid of this place, Lola."

"There must be a way."

A truck pulled up at the gas pumps and I went out and serviced the truck.

When I was through, the trucker said he would have breakfast, and after he had gone, other truckers arrived. I didn't get a chance to talk any more with Lola. As soon as she had put the pies in the oven, she got changed and told me she was going.

"I'll be back by lunch time. Don't forget the pies."

I watched her drive away, then went into the kitchen to wash up the various breakfast things.

I was feeling pretty good. Now the subject of the money had come out in the open my final uneasiness that she was putting on an act disappeared.

I had to concentrate in earnest on how we were to leave Point of No Return so that no one would suspect anything was wrong.

But the more I thought about it, the tighter the trap became. We couldn't sell the place as it was in Jenson's name. We couldn't give out that Jenson was dead. We couldn't sneak away and leave the place deserted. The police would move in, and it wouldn't take them long to find Jenson's body, then there would be a murder hunt for both of us.

The more I wrestled with the problem the more complicated it became. Then I saw suddenly there was no safe way out. We were in a trap and the doors of the trap were shut. If we hoped to remain safe, we had to stay on in this isolated place for keeps. We just didn't dare leave.

While all this was going on in my mind, I was pacing up and down in the lunch room. The sound of a car pulling up made me look out of the window. I was in time to see Ricks get out of his battered car, followed by his dog. He shambled into the repair shed.

With my heart thumping, I went across to the shed fast.

I found Ricks wandering aimlessly around, looking at the tools. His dog kept close to his heels, and as I came in, the dog cringed, moving even closer to its master and looking at me mournfully with its bloodshot eyes.

"What do you want?" I said, making my voice hard and tough.

Ricks paused and squinted at me, shoving the dog away with his leg.

"You heard from my brother-in-law?"

"No."

"Is she around?"

"If you mean Mrs. Jenson . . . she's in Wentworth this morning. What do you want?"

I saw the dog suddenly turn its head and stare at the workbench that stood over Jenson's grave. It moved forward to the bench and began sniffing at the ground.

I felt sudden chills start up my spine.

"I'm still without my pension," Ricks said. "I'm running out of money."

"I can't help that."

Tentatively, the dog began to scratch at the ground, then finding the ground loose, it began to dig in earnest.

Ricks turned and stared at the dog.

"Well, I'll be darned! I've never seen Caesar do a thing like that before." He moved forward and gave the dog a solid kick on its rump, sending it squealing to the door of the shed. "I'm down to my last buck," he went on to me. "How about lending me something? As soon as I've got my pension I'll pay it back."

As he talked the dog crept back again, looking furtively at its master, then it began to dig again.

"Watch your damned dog!" I shouted, and picking up a block of wood, I threw it at the dog, sending it yelping once more to the door.

Ricks glared at me.

"That's no way to treat a poor dumb animal! You should be ashamed of yourself!"

"Get out of here! You and your damned dog!" I snarled.

Ricks was now staring at the hole the dog had dug, a puzzled expression on his face.

"Have you been burying something there?"

I felt cold sweat break out on my face.

"No . . . come on! Beat it!"

Instead, he shambled over to the hole and knelt down, staring at it.

"Well, someone's been digging here." He pushed his dirty, claw-like hand into the loose earth. As if it recognised co-operation, the dog came up, wagging its tail and whining, then it began to dig again.

Impatiently, Ricks shoved it away.

"Maybe Carl has buried his money here," he muttered. "He would be fool enough to do just that. How about taking a look? Got a spade?"

I was now in a hell of a panic. I moved forward and there must have been an expression in my eyes that told Ricks I meant trouble. He straightened up hastily and backed away.

"Okay, okay, fella, no need to get mad," he whined, still backing away, his dog following him. "Just a thought that dropped into my mind. Think nothing of it."

"Get out and stay away from here!" I shouted at him. "Go on! Get out!"

"How about lending me five bucks?" he whined, still backing away, he was now out in the hot sunshine.

"You're getting nothing out of me," I said, moving after him. "Beat it!"

By now he was close to his battered car. He paused, his hand on the car door and he squinted at me.

"Okay, if that's the way you want it, fella," he said, a sudden rasp in his voice. "I'm going to talk to the cops! I'm going to tell them to look for Carl! You and that whore, cuddling and kissing . . ."

I jumped him. My fist slammed against his jaw, sending him flat on his back. I was so mad I didn't notice a trucker had just pulled up by the gas pumps. It was only when he yelled at me I got control of myself. I was about ready to give this skinny vulture the hiding of his life.

As soon as the dog saw its master sprawl in the dust, it fled, shivering into the car.

The trucker got out of the truck and hurried over, his expression aggressive.

"Hey! If you want to hit a guy, pick one your own age and size!" he bawled at me.

I felt tempted to take him, but I knew it would be bad for business. Truckers talk together. I choked down my rage and stepped back as Ricks crawled unsteadily to his feet.

"Okay, okay," I said to the trucker. "You're right. I guess I blew my top and I'm sorry, but this punk comes scrounging here week after week and he drives me nuts."

The trucker lost his aggressive look.

"Well, yeah . . . but to hit an old guy . . ." He stared at Ricks, then grimaced. "A scrounger, huh?"

"You said it. He never stops putting the bite on me."

He relaxed, nodding.

"Sorry I pushed my oar in. My father-in-law is the same. I could do with some gas."

"Sure. I'm coming."

He went back to his truck. Ricks got slowly and painfully into his car. He was holding his jaw and mumbling to himself.

I took from my wallet a ten dollar bill and shoved it at him.

"Here . . . take this and beat it," I said.

He had started the car engine. With a shaking hand, he took the bill, then crumpling it, he threw it in my face.

"I'll fix you for this!" he snarled, his face vicious with rage. "I'm going to talk to the police."

He stamped down on the gas pedal and the car shot crazily away.

Then I knew I had made a dangerous mistake hitting him. I had imagined he was so spineless and such a scrounger I could pay for that punch with a ten dollar bill.

I picked up the bill and put it back in my wallet. There was a chill of fear around my heart.

I walked over to the waiting trucker and filled his tank. He looked curiously at me. He had seen Ricks throw the money at me, but he didn't say anything.

When he had gone, I went into the repair shed and dragged the workbench away from Jenson's grave. Working fast, I filled in the hole dug by Ricks's dog and levelled the ground. Then drawing from a pile of rusty scrap that stood against the far wall, I made a great heap of it on the grave.

The job took me half an hour, but when I was through, there was no chance of the dog pulling the same trick on me again.

While I worked, I wondered about Ricks. Would he go to the police? In the vicious mood he was in, he probably would, but would they pay any attention to him? If they came out here and investigated me I was sunk. Should I pack up and get out while the going was good?

Still trying to make up my mind, I left the repair shed and went over to the lunch room.

I saw a dusty Lincoln beside the gas pumps. I had been so preoccupied with my thoughts I hadn't seen it arrive.

There was a man sitting at the wheel, and there was something familiar about him.

He got out of the car and came towards me. He was wearing a shabby, wrinkled suit. A slouch hat that had seen some years' hard wear rested at the back of his head.

I recognised him, and my heart skipped a beat and then began to race.

The man walking towards me was Roy Tracey.

CHAPTER TEN

I

Roy recognised me at the same time as I recognised him. He came to an abrupt halt and I saw him change colour.

We stood staring at each other.

He was the first to recover. The colour came back to his face, his mouth twisted into that old cynical grin I knew so well. He started towards me at a run.

"Chet! Is it really you? Am I glad to see you!"

We were shaking hands and thumping each other. It wasn't until this moment that I fully realised how much I had missed him: how lonely I had been these months for his company.

"You son of a gun!" I said and hugged him. "Is it good to see you again?"

He caught hold of my shoulders and shoved me back at arm's length while he stared searchingly at me.

"What are you doing here? I thought you were out of the country?"

"I hope the police think so too," I said. I was so pleased to see him I felt like crying. "Come on in and have a drink." I grabbed him by the arm and led him into the lunch room. "Where did you drop from?"

"Little Creek . . . what a dump that is!" He sat on a stool by the counter and looked around. "But what are you doing here?"

I began to make two highballs.

"It's the perfect hide-out, Roy. I work here now."

"It sure is, but wouldn't it be better if you were in Mexico or Canada?"

I gave him one of the drinks.

"Easier said than done. I hadn't any money. I was lucky to find this place."

"You really think you're safe here?"

"I can't be really safe anywhere in the jam I'm in."

He reached over and patted my arm.

"I read about the escape. That took guts! I've never ceased to think about you. I never thought I'd see you again."

I grinned at him. "That makes two of us."

He looked at me, his hand sliding down my arm and gripping my wrist.

"This is the first chance I've had, Chet, to thank you for what you did for me. I'll never forget it! The way you covered me . . ."

"Forget it. You would have done the same for me."

"You're damn right I would, but it's something I'll never forget. When they caught you . . ." He blew out his cheeks. "What a sweat I was in! I thought they were bound to pick me up. You're a pal: a real pal."

"You were a lot smarter than I was," I said. "Why should we both go into the hole? If I had gone with you instead of panicking . . ."

He took a long drink.

"You weren't the only one in a panic. Gee! I nearly blew my top! I guess we were nuts to have pulled that job. I've never stopped regretting it."

"Me too. What are you doing here anyway? What brings you out here?"

He finished his drink, then pushed the glass towards me. I made two more drinks as he said, "I'm on the road. That's a laugh, isn't it? This is the big squeeze. They want me out of the lousy firm now. They have an idea I was mixed up in that business with you. Franklin hinted that the big wheels upstairs were pretty sure I was in it with you. They knew what pals we were, and someone let out I was in the hole for five hundred bucks. So I was taken off safe work. They said they thought it was a sound idea for me to get some experience selling these goddamn safes instead of repairing them. They gave me a list of customers that have old models, and my job now is to persuade them to buy new ones." He took from his pocket book a slip of paper. "Point of No Return. Carl Jenson, proprietor. Is that right? He has an old Lawrence safe here. It's my job to sell him a new one. Is he your boss?"

At that moment a Cadillac pulled up by the gas pumps and the driver hit the horn impatiently.

"I'll be right back," I said, glad of the interruption. I wanted a few moments to decide just how much I was going to tell him.

While I served the Caddy, my mind was busy. I decided I couldn't tell Roy the whole story. I couldn't tell him about Jenson's death. That was Lola's secret, not mine.

I decided to tell him the story I was telling everyone else: that Jenson was away, looking for another filling station, and he wouldn't be back for a couple of months.

I returned to the lunch room.

Roy was smoking and wandering around staring at everything as I came in.

"This is certainly a swell set-up, Chet. I envy you. It must be a little gold mine."

"It's not so lousy," I said. "Carl Jenson's away. I don't reckon he'll be back for a while."

Roy pulled a face.

"You mean I've come all this way for nothing? How about his wife? Could she buy a safe?"

"Not a chance. Jenson is the boss around here. You're out of luck."

He finished his drink, then leaning forward he carefully deposited ash into the ash tray on the counter. "I'll tell you something. I'm a lousy salesman. I've been on this job now seven weeks and I haven't sold one goddamn safe yet." He looked at me, frowning. "At the end of the month my sales report is going to look like a hole in the ground, and then the axe will fall. I'm not kidding myself. I'm going to be out of a job pretty soon."

"You should worry. It beats me why you let them push you around. Why don't you go to Carringtons or Haywards? Their safes are miles ahead of Lawrences, and they would jump at you."

He shook his head.

"That's where you're wrong. They would want to know why I had quit and Franklin would give them the hint. He wouldn't say I had been mixed up in that business, but he could and would say I wasn't considered a good risk, and that would be that."

I stared at him.

"But they can't prove it, Roy."

"They don't have to. All they have to do is to drop a hint."

"So what are you going to do?"

He shrugged his shoulders.

"I don't know. I'm a good safe man and I can fix locks, but I'm not much good at anything else. Besides, I'm thirty-five. It comes tough to change your job at that age and get away with it." He looked at his watch. "Getting on for lunch time. I'm hungry. How about something to eat?"

I gave him the menu as two truckers came in. They sat on stools away from us and ordered hamburgers.

As I was preparing the hamburgers, Roy asked how the fried chicken was.

"Okay," I said. "You have that with green salad and the cranberry pie and you'll know you have eaten."

"Fine."

A boy and a girl drove up in an M.G. sports and came in. The boy asked if the lunch was ready.

I said there was fried chicken and they settled for that.

Every so often I looked through the window for the sight of
Lola. As I was dishing up the chicken I saw the Mercury come
over the hill.

I put the plate of chicken before Roy.

"Mrs. Jenson is coming now," I said, and lowering my voice,
I went on, "I'm known here as Patmore, Roy. Don't forget it."

He nodded and winked.

Lola drove around to the back and I heard her come in through
the kitchen entrance. I went into the kitchen.

"I'm a little late," she said. "Are you all right? Anyone wanting
food?"

"It's under control." I put my arm around her and kissed her.
"Something's blown up, Lola. A guy I knew in the past has
dropped in. It's okay. I can trust him. He wanted to do business
with your husband. I've told him he won't be back for a couple
of months."

Lola looked startled.

"Are you sure you can trust him, Chet?"

"Yes, he's my best friend. It's okay."

I heard someone tapping impatiently on the counter of the
lunch room.

"I'd better get back. We can unload the stuff later."

I left her and returned to the lunch room.

There was a guy standing at the counter: short, fat and wearing a fawn seersucker suit.

"I have a party of twenty outside," he said. "Can you feed
them?"

"Sure," I said. "Wheel them in."

Through the window I could see a luxury rubberneck bus
parked by the pumps. It was loaded with tourists.

I put my head around the kitchen door and warned Lola there
was a rush on the way. She nodded. No rush ever fazed her.

The lunch room got crowded, and although Lola and I worked
at top pressure, there was some delay. Then a couple of trucks
pulled up and the truckers honked for gas.

Roy had finished his meal and was watching me trying to
handle the rush. He slid off the stool and came over to me.

"How about me helping out?" he said. "I can handle the
pumps. Okay?"

"Fine—go ahead."

I reached under the counter and gave him the satchel containing the change. "You'll get the price off the pumps—they are all
automatic."

He took the satchel and went out to the pumps.

For the next hour and a half we were all kept hard at it. Finally,
the tourists left, and the place suddenly became empty. I had been

so busy I hadn't had time to see how Roy had been making out. Now I went to the window as Lola came out of the kitchen.

Roy was on the job. He had three cars in a row waiting for gas. He worked quickly, washing the windshields as the pump was working.

Lola joined me.

"What goes on?" she asked, watching Roy. "Who's that?"

"That's Roy Tracey: the guy I was telling you about, he offered to help out. Looks like he's doing pretty well."

"He certainly does."

There was a note in her voice that made me look at her. She was studying Roy, her green eyes slightly narrowed.

"He wouldn't want a job here, Chet?" she said. "We need help, and if you can trust him . . ."

I put my arm around her and gave her a little hug.

"I was going to suggest it. That guy and I are like brothers. We can trust him, Lola. I told him Jenson was away. We can tell him he's gone off with some woman and you and I are living together. He'll understand. But maybe he wouldn't want to stay on here. He's restless. Maybe it would be too lonely for him." I grinned at her. "At least, he won't make any passes at you. Since his marriage broke up he isn't interested in women."

She looked at me.

"He's coming now. Ask him, Chet."

The screen door pushed open and Roy came in. He paused in the doorway and stared at Lola. I saw a surprised look come into his eyes. Even in her soiled overalls she was still a woman to stare at, but that didn't bother me.

"Roy, this is Mrs. Jenson," I said. "Lola, this is Roy Tracey."

"I see you have been helping out, Mr. Tracey," Lola said. smiling. "Thanks. We had quite a rush on."

Roy grinned at her.

"I'll say you did! I enjoyed helping. Nice place you have here, Mrs. Jenson."

"You like it?"

"I certainly do."

"How about staying on then, Roy?" I said. "There's a cabin across the way. You can have that. The job's worth forty a week. How about it?"

Roy looked from me to Lola, his grin widening.

"Are you sure you want me?" He was speaking to Lola. "If you do, I'd jump at it."

"We were only saying the other day we would have to get help," Lola said.

"Then it's a deal."

A Ford station wagon rolled out of the dust and pulled up by the pumps.

"Want me to take care of it, boss?" Roy said, grinning at me.

"I'll handle it," I said. "You two get acquainted." I looked at Lola. "This guy went to school with me. Treat him nicely. We're like brothers."

Roy gave me a light punch on the chest.

"That's right." He looked directly at Lola. "Like brothers."

II

It wasn't until after ten when things had slackened off that we three sat down to supper. It seemed odd to have Roy opposite me and Lola on my right.

Roy was enthusiastic about the job. .

"This is certainly some place!" he said. "Boy! Am I glad I walked in the way I did! This is a lot better than selling safes."

We were eating Lola's famous spaghetti and veal cutlets. Lola, her spaghetti neatly rolled up on her fork, paused to look at him.

"Is that your line—safes?" she asked.

"I'll have you know, Mrs. Jenson," Roy said, grinning at me, "Chet and I are the two best safe men in the country. That's right, isn't it, Chet?"

"Well, we're not so lousy. I've known worse."

"Chet and I started in the same business on the same day," Roy said to Lola. "He is a better safe man than I am, but I'm better at locks. The trouble with him is he is too conscientious. Ever since I've known him he's pulled me out of jams. Usually, I get him into a mess and he gets me out of it."

"You're going to find it pretty quiet here, Roy," I said. "There's not much to do except work."

"It'll suit me," he said, his expression suddenly serious, "but what will Mr. Jenson say when he comes back and finds he has another mouth to feed?" He looked at Lola. "I would like to think this is a permanent job, Mrs. Jenson."

"I'm not sure he is coming back," Lola said, picking up her cue fast.

Roy blinked.

"Is that a fact?" He looked quickly at me, then at her. "Some trouble?"

"The usual." She made it sound very casual. "I haven't told anyone yet, but I don't think he's coming back. He's found someone he likes better than me."

Roy looked embarrassed.

"I'm sorry . . ."

She smiled at him.

"You don't have to be." She reached out and put her hand on mine. "You see, Chet and I . . ." She stopped and squeezed my hand. "At least my husband left me this place—and Chet."

Roy shook his head wonderingly at me.

"What a guy! Talk about luck!"

"That's the way it is." I pushed back my chair. "Come over to the cabin, Roy. You may as well get settled in."

Roy stood up.

"Thanks for the swell meal, Mrs. Jenson."

She smiled up at him.

"You'd better call me Lola. We're not formal here."

"Okay. How about helping with the dishes?"

"I'll do it. You go with Chet."

As we walked across the moonlit sand to the cabin, Roy said, "Some chick! I'm glad for you, Chet. You're sure I won't be in the way?"

"Of course not. The one thing this place lacks for me has been male company."

I unlocked the cabin door and we went in.

"This is pretty good," Roy said, looking around. "Even a TV set." He moved to the window and looked across at the bungalow. "Is that where you are?"

"Where else do you think I'd be?"

"Yeah—your way with women." He lit a cigarette, then dumping his bag on a chair, he began to unpack. "This guy Jenson must have been nuts to have walked out of here for a woman. I can't figure it. Seems to me his wife has it all—what more does he want?"

"It's my guess he's settled for some fat, comfortable woman of his own age," I said. "Lola is twenty years younger than he is, and she isn't all that easy to live with."

Roy drew on his cigarette, sucked down smoke, then exhaled in a long, steady stream.

"Why didn't he get rid of her then and keep this place for himself?"

Roy was no fool. I could see he was puzzled by the set-up. I had to convince him or he might begin to suspect the truth.

"That's easier said than done," I said. "You can't just get rid of your wife when you happen to feel like it."

His dark, quizzing eyes searched my face.

"How long has he been gone?"

"Four or five weeks."

"And she's heard nothing from him?"

"No."

"She doesn't know for certain there is another woman?"

"She's pretty sure."

He shook his head.

"But he could walk in here at any moment and catch you in bed with her?"

"He's not coming back, Roy."

He looked sharply at me, then away.

"Does she know you're in this fix, Chet?"

"Yes. I told her."

He had emptied his bag by now. His things were scattered on the bed.

"This place must be quite a gold mine. What's the weekly take?"

The take had been less than I had expected it would be. Jenson had made his money from his scrap deals. This I had discovered after the first week of his death. Scrap was something I didn't understand, nor did Lola. Since Jenson's hand had come off the wheel, the scrap trade had come to a standstill. Lola and I had had to rely on what the lunch room, the gas pumps and the repair shed brought in. This turned out to be a lot less than I had thought. We made a net profit of around 200 dollars a week, and this we divided: half for her, half for me.

With nothing to spend my share on, I had put it every week in the safe to accumulate with the rest of my savings. What she did with hers I didn't ask.

"It's not as good as you might think—around two hundred a week."

Roy pulled a face.

"You surprise me. I'd have thought it would be a lot more." He crossed to the window and looked out. "There must be ways of turning a set-up like this into big money, Chet."

"You're wrong. It's too off the beaten track."

"But that's the whole point." He looked steadily at me. "This is just the place for some kind of racket. You can see that, can't you?"

"What do you mean?"

"You don't want to stay here buried for the rest of your days. You and I have always been after the big money. We could dream up something that would turn this place into a gold mine."

I sat on the bed, frowning at him.

"Dream up—what?"

"I'm just coasting, but how about the Mexican emigrants? You could land them here at two hundred bucks a head. It's the ideal place for them. Have you thought of that?"

"If you had been in Farnworth for a couple of months, Roy," I said quietly, "you wouldn't talk this way."

He ran his fingers through his hair and grinned uneasily at me.

"Yeah, I know how you feel. We handled that job wrong. We acted like a couple of dopes. We should have watched that guy Cooper for at least a week. We should have found out what his habits really were. We handled that job badly."

"We shouldn't have handled it at all. We asked for trouble and we got it—at least I did. Let's get this straight, I'm through with rackets of any kind."

"I understand that, but I've still got the money itch. Sooner or later I've got to get my hands on a big slice of money. If I don't get it soon, I'll never get it."

"You're not going to get it here; make up your mind about that," I said.

He shrugged, then grinned.

"Well, okay. So we're through with rackets." He went over to the chest of drawers and pulled open a drawer. "Just so long as I know." He dumped some shirts into the drawer, then he looked at me. "Haven't you the urge to make big money any more, Chet?"

"No," I said. "Farnworth cured me. If you had been there, it would have cured you too."

"Pretty tough, huh?" He took a collection of handkerchiefs and socks off the bed, pulled open the second drawer and tumbled them in. Then he said sharply, "Hell! What's this?"

The tone of his voice made me stiffen.

"What's what?"

He put his hand into the drawer and lifted out the .45 Colt that had shot Jenson. I had forgotten I had put it into the drawer after Lola had killed Jenson. I had forgotten it even existed.

The sight of the gun in Roy's hand turned me cold. I made a movement to snatch it from him, but just managed to control myself.

"That's Jenson's," I said, trying to make my voice sound casual. "I found it when he left."

Roy was staring at the gun. He spun the cylinder, then he sniffed at the barrel.

"This has been fired recently," he said. He drew out the empty cartridge case and dropped it on the bed. "Did you know that?" He looked searching at me. "Who got killed, Chet?"

It was an effort for me to meet that stare, but I did it.

"No one got killed," I said. "Jenson used to shoot at hawks. He must have forgotten to clean the gun."

"Shooting hawks with a .45?" Roy put the gun down on the top of the chest. "He must have been some shot."

"He never hit anything." I went over and picked up the gun, shoving it into my hip pocket. "Well, it's getting late. I guess I'll turn in. You got everything?"

"Couldn't be better." There was a flat note in his voice that made me uneasy. "How about night work? What happens?"

"We'll take it in turns. I'm on tonight. You can take tomorrow night."

"Fine. Well, it's been good—this talk. It's wonderful to see you again, Chet. I can't believe my good luck."

I slapped him on the shoulder.

"Nor can I." I was now at the door. "Get a good sleep."

"I sure will . . . and Chet . . ."

I paused.

He rubbed his jaw as he stared at me.

"Yeah?"

"Clean that gun. A dirty gun is a dangerous thing to leave lying around."

I couldn't meet his eyes.

"You're right. Well . . . so long . . ."

"So long, pal."

I went out of the cabin. Seeing no lights on in the lunch room, but a light on in Lola's bedroom, I walked over to the bungalow.

Lola was in her bra and panties, sitting on the bed. As I came in, she began to strip off her stockings.

"Gee! I'm tired," she said, yawning. "I like your friend, Chet."

"Yes, he's the best." I took the gun from my hip pocket and put it in the top drawer of the chest. Her back was to me and she didn't see me do it. I told myself I would clean the gun tomorrow. "We three will get along all right. You know, it's a funny thing, but Roy isn't interested in women. It beats me, but since he married and since she walked out on him, he has never looked at another woman."

Lola got up and took off the rest of her clothes. She reached for her nightdress while I watched her.

As she slipped the nightdress on, she said, "Every man is interested in a woman—it depends on the woman."

"I've known him for thirty years," I said. "There was only one woman—the one he married, and he was sick of her in a couple of years."

Lola got into bed.

"She couldn't have been much." She raised her arms above her head, stretching and yawning. "You'll be in by one, Chet?"

"Yes." I came over to her and kissed her. "Sleep well. I'll try not to disturb you."

"You won't. I feel dead." She pulled the bedclothes up to her chin and smiled at me. "I forgot to ask you—everything all right while I've been away?"

I felt a little kick under my heart. I had forgotten Ricks. The

118

excitement of meeting Roy had put that thin vulture right out of my mind.

Lola saw my change of expression and she sat up abruptly.

"What is it, Chet?"

"Ricks was here this afternoon. He needled me into hitting him."

"You hit him?"

Her voice shot up a note.

"I hit him. I had to."

She gripped my arm.

"Tell me! What happened?"

I told her. She sat bolt upright in bed, the bedclothes clutched to her, her green eyes wide as she listened.

"I offered him ten bucks," I concluded, "and he threw them at me. He said he was going to talk to the cops."

She dropped back on the pillow.

"He won't," she said. "Even if he did, they know what a scrounging rat he is. They won't listen to him."

"I hope you're right."

"You were crazy to hit him, Chet."

"I know. Well, we'll see."

"I'm sure they won't listen to him."

I bent and kissed her.

"Go to sleep. I'll be in around one o'clock."

"Tomorrow night we'll go to bed early and let Roy look after the place."

I ran my fingers through her silky hair.

"That's a date," I said.

CHAPTER ELEVEN

I

IT was while we were having breakfast that I told Roy about Ricks.

"You have got to watch out for him," I said. "He's always dropping in unexpectedly. He was in yesterday, and he needled me into socking him. It was a damn silly thing to do but I did it. He talked of going to the police."

Roy looked up sharply.

"The police? Why?"

"He caught Lola and me fooling around together. He doesn't know Jenson has gone off with some woman. He wants to find him and make trouble."

Roy finished his coffee and lit a cigarette. We were eating alone. Lola hadn't got up yet.

"Why doesn't Lola tell him that Jenson isn't coming back?"

"For one thing it isn't his business," I said. "For another, he wouldn't believe it."

"I can imagine that." Roy shook his head. "It certainly foxes me that a guy could be so dumb as to leave a set-up like this and a wife who can cook as well as she can."

"If he comes around when we're not here, Roy, watch him. Don't let him have a thing and don't tell him anything."

"Will he talk to the cops?"

"No. Even if he does, they wouldn't listen to him." I stood up. "How about giving me a hand? This place has to be cleaned every morning. I guess Lola's taking advantage of the new hand. She's still in bed."

While we set about cleaning the lunch room, Roy said, "Tell me about Farnworth, Chet. How did you manage to get away? They said in the papers you're the first man who has got out and survived."

I told him.

He was so fascinated that he leaned on the broom handle, listening, and every now and then he shook his head in wonderment.

"Gee! You've got guts!" he said when I had finished. "I'm damned if I would have risked those dogs."

"You would have risked anything to have got away from that place," I said. "I'm not going back. I would rather be dead."

Roy grimaced.

"You should be safe here. You're a long way from Farnworth. Who would think of looking for you here?"

"That's the way I figure it."

Through the window I caught sight of Lola coming over from the bungalow. She was wearing her halter and shorts. She had piled her red hair to the top of her head and had caught it back with a strip of green ribbon.

I felt a sudden stab of uneasiness at the sight of her. She hadn't worn that get-up for weeks. Now, when another male was on the scene, she had suddenly decided to show off her body. I looked quickly at Roy, who was polishing the counter.

Lola came in, smiling. She made quite an entrance.

"Hello," she said. "That's what I like to see—my two slaves hard at work."

I was watching Roy. He paused, looked up and stared at her. She was leaning against the door post, looking directly at him. I've never seen her look so provocatively sexy and attractive.

Roy's expression didn't change. He just stared indifferently at her, then went on polishing the counter.

"Hello there," he said. "Are we the only two who work around here?"

I saw her expression harden. This wasn't the reception she had expected. She had anticipated that Roy would have reacted to this display of feminine charm. I relaxed, turning away so she couldn't see my smile of satisfaction. It was still the same Roy: women meant nothing to him.

She walked across to the kitchen door. There she paused to look at Roy again, but he had his back to her and he was whistling under his breath. She went into the kitchen and slammed the door.

Roy winked at me.

"Women . . . I don't know," he said. "They're never satisfied."

"It was my fault," I said. "I told her you weren't interested in women. She couldn't believe it. Maybe she will now."

A truck pulled up by the gas pumps and the driver honked on his horn.

"I'll take care of it," Roy said, and he went out to the truck.

I went into the kitchen.

Lola looked sulky. She had put on her overall and was busy preparing chickens for the spit.

"Let's go to the movies tonight, Chet," she said. "Roy can look after the place. We can catch the midnight performance. We'll be back here by three."

I hesitated. I wasn't sure if it was safe for us to be seen together in Wentworth.

"Maybe we'd better wait, Lola . . ."

She turned quickly, her expression hardening.

"Wait for what?"

"No one knows the story yet. Sooner or later we'll have to put out the rumour Jenson has walked out of here, but until we do, maybe it would be safer for us not to be seen together."

"I'm sick and tired of having my fun alone," she said. "I want to go to the movies tonight and I want you to go with me."

"Well, okay, then we'll go. It'll be dark. The chances are no one will spot us."

"But, Chet, it doesn't matter if anyone does spot us," she said impatiently. "It's our business—not theirs."

"Have you forgotten he's buried here? If the police came out here and started to dig . . ."

"If the moon was made of green cheese! Do you think I'm going to spend the rest of my days being scared of the police?"

"You can talk. You haven't been in Farnworth."

Then Roy came in.

"Chet and I are going to the movies tonight," Lola said to him. "Can you manage alone? We'll go after the dinner hour. It'll just mean serving gas and some sandwiches."

Roy glanced at me. He looked surprised.

"Why, sure I'll manage fine."

She turned away and began putting the chickens on the spit.

"If you have a minute, Chet," Roy went on, "I'd be glad if you would take a look at my car. It's missing on damn near every plug. I never was any good with cars."

"I'll fix it," I said. "It's time you learned to fix a car. What's going to happen if Lola and me go to the movies and you get a breakdown?"

He grinned.

"I'll have a breakdown on my hands," he said.

He went to the kitchen door ahead of me, and pushed it open, then he paused abruptly—so abruptly I nearly cannoned into him.

"Look who's here!"

I looked beyond him through the lunch room window.

A car had just pulled up. There were two men in it: both wearing Stetson hats and dark suits. One of them, big, fat with a pot belly, got out of the car, leaving the other at the wheel. The sun glittered on the star he wore on his lapel. As he squeezed himself out of the car, his coat fell open. I saw the gun belt and the .45 in its holster.

"Cops!" Roy said sharply.

I felt a chill snake up my spine. I looked wildly at Lola. It was a funny thing but in this moment of panic I turned to her, feeling she and no one else could save me.

"It's the sheriff," I said. "He's coming in here!"

Lola picked up a cloth and wiped her hands.

"I'll handle him," she said. She was as calm and as unruffled as a bishop presiding at a tea party. "It's all right, Chet."

It was easy for her to be calm. She hadn't to face Farnworth. The sight of that fat sheriff froze my blood.

Both Roy and I stood aside and we watched her walk into the lunch room. As the door swung to behind her, I heard her say, "Why, hello, Sheriff, you're quite a stranger."

I felt sweat on my face as I leaned against the wall, listening. Roy stood on the other side of the door, also listening and watching me.

"Hello there, Mrs. Jenson, nice to see you again." The sheriff had a booming voice that carried easily to us. "Is Mr. Jenson around? I wanted a word with him."

"Why, no. Carl is away."

Lola's voice sounded casual. I imagined her facing the sheriff, her green eyes bland and her expression unruffled. It would take a lot more than a fat sheriff to rattle her, but he was certainly rattling me.

"Mr. Jenson—away?" His voice registered his startled surprise. "That's an event, isn't it? I've never known him to leave here before. Where can I find him?"

"I don't know." She managed to convey by the tone of her voice that she didn't care either. "He's moving around—anyway, that's what he told me. He is supposed to be either in Arizona or Colorado. Since he left, I haven't heard a word from him."

"Any idea when he'll be back, Mrs. Jenson?"

A pause, then she said in a cold, flat voice, "I don't think he is coming back."

I heard the sheriff's grunt of surprise.

"Not coming back? What do you mean?"

"He's walked out on me."

There was a long pause. I could imagine him staring at her and getting a blank stare in return. I looked across at Roy, who was listening with the same intenseness as I was. Our eyes met. He frowned, shaking his head.

The sheriff said, "Well, this is a surprise. What makes you say that, Mrs. Jenson?"

"It's not the first time a husband has found someone else he likes better than his wife." She managed now to get a waspish note in her voice. "What business is it of yours anyway, Sheriff? If Carl likes to make a fool of himself over some woman, that's my headache, not yours."

I heard him shuffle his feet.

"That's a fact, Mrs. Jenson, but I'm sorry to hear it. Some woman, huh?"

"Oh, I suppose it is as much my fault as his. I shouldn't have married him. He was too old for me. From the start we didn't get along together. Well, at least he did the decent thing: he left me this place. I won't starve. What did you want to see him about? Anything I can do?"

The sheriff cleared his throat noisily.

"I understand there's a fella working here—Jack Patmore. Is that right?"

My heart began to thump violently. I looked quickly around the kitchen for a weapon. There was a meat cleaver lying on the table. I reached out and grabbed it. I wasn't going back to Farnworth. If this fat sheriff imagined he could take me, he was in for a surprise.

Roy, watching me, shook his head. He had lost colour. Maybe he could see from the expression on my face that I wasn't going to be arrested without a fight. Maybe the sight of the sheriff's gun scared him: it didn't me. I would rather be shot than face Farnworth.

I heard Lola say, "Patmore? Why, yes. He works here. Carl hired him before he left. I have to have someone here to help out."

"I understand that, Mrs. Jenson. I want to talk to him."

"I'm not stopping you." Her voice was very casual. "He's somewhere around."

Roy moved silently over to me.

"I can handle this," he whispered. "Leave it to me."

He crossed the kitchen to the back door, opened it and moved quickly and silently out into the hot sunshine.

Lola was saying, "He's probably over the way in the repair shed. Why not see for yourself?"

"I guess I'll do that, Mrs. Jenson."

I heard the sheriff move to the door, then Lola said, "Did George Ricks tell you about Patmore, Sheriff?"

"That's right . . . he did."

"Did he complain that Patmore hit him?"

There was a pause, then the sheriff said awkwardly, "Why, yes."

Lola went on, her voice hard, "Did he happen to tell you why Patmore hit him?"

"This Patmore seems a quarrelsome type. Ricks said . . ."

"He didn't tell you that Patmore hit him because Ricks called me a whore?" The indignation in her voice sounded very sincere. "I would like to think, Sheriff, you would have hit Ricks if you had heard him call me that."

The sheriff cleared his throat.

"Why, yes. The fact is I had an idea he was shooting the breeze . . ."

I heard the screen door creak open, then Roy's voice say, "Morning, Sheriff."

A pause, then the sheriff said, "Is your name Jack Patmore?"

"That's correct," Roy said.

I leaned against the door, listening.

Roy was about my height, dark like me, and his moustache was clipped like mine. If Ricks had given the sheriff a description of me, Roy could be mistaken for me.

The sheriff said in his heavy, booming voice, "George Ricks says you knocked him down yesterday. That right?"

Lola was quick to cue Roy in.

"I was telling the Sheriff," she said, "you hit Ricks because he called me a whore."

"I certainly did," Roy said. He sounded cheerful. "And I'll tell you something else, Sheriff. If Ricks shows his snout here in the future, I'll not only knock him down again, but I'll kick his backside as well."

There was a pause, then the sheriff said, "Where do you come from, Patmore?"

My heart began to thump again and my grip tightened on the handle of the meat cleaver.

Roy said, a jeering note in his voice, "Oakville, California. In case you don't know, Sheriff, in my home town we don't let rats like Ricks call women names. If you want my fingerprints just tell me—you can have them."

"Okay, fella, you don't have to act smart." The sheriff sounded annoyed. "It's my job to know who lives around in this district."

"Carl met Patmore in his scrap deals," Lola said quickly. "That's why he hired him to work for him."

There was a pause, then the sheriff said, "Well, all right. Take my tip, Patmore, don't be quite so free with your fists in the future."

"You tell Ricks to watch his dirty mouth and I'll watch my fists," Roy said. "How's that?"

The sheriff said, after hesitation, "I'll talk to him."

"And while you're talking to him," Lola broke in, "Perhaps you'll be good enough to tell him to keep away from here. He does nothing but pester me for money."

"I can imagine, Mrs. Jenson. Your husband told me about him —if there ever was a scrounger . . ." Again the long pause, then he

125

went on, "I'm sorry to hear you and Mr. Jenson . . ." He cleared his throat. "Well, I hope it will clear up."

"That's kind of you," Lola said indifferently, "but you mustn't worry about Carl nor me. Carl is happy, so am I."

"I'm glad to hear it." His voice sounded anything but glad. "We'll miss Mr. Jenson. I would never have believed he would have walked out of here—he was born here."

"It seems some women can make the nicest man act like a fool." There was a waspish note in her voice again. "This place isn't my idea of paradise. I don't plan to stay here longer than I can help. When I've saved enough money I'm leaving. If Carl bothers to let me know where he is, I'll suggest he either comes back here or lets me sell the place. One thing I'm sure of—I'm not spending the rest of my days here."

"Well, I can understand that, Mrs. Jenson. If your husband isn't coming back, I can see you wouldn't want to stay on here. It's a lonely place for a woman."

"Yes. Well, it's been nice seeing you again, Sheriff."

"I'm sorry I don't have the time to come out here more often. It's a long way out, but if you ever want any help, you have only to call me."

"I'll remember that—thanks."

I heard him walk heavily to the door.

"So long, Patmore."

"So long, Sheriff," Roy said.

I heard the door click, then the car start up and drive away.

I put the meat cleaver down on the table and wiped the sweat off my face.

Lola and Roy came in.

"That was pretty smart," I said to Roy. "I thought I was really in a jam that time."

"I told you I could handle him," Lola said impatiently. "You didn't have to get so worked up."

"I don't know about that," Roy put in. "I would have been worked up all right if I'd been Chet."

"Oh, you men!" She started work on the chickens again. "You fuss about anything."

Roy started towards the door, grinning at me.

"Thanks, Roy," I said. "That was pretty smart."

"As if I didn't owe you something, pal," he said, and went out.

There was a long pause while I watched Lola arranging the chickens on the spit.

"This washes out tonight, Lola," I said.

She turned quickly to stare at me, frowning.

"What do you mean?"

"I'm not going into Wentworth."

126

"Why not?"

"Use your head, will you?" I said, getting angry with her. "Suppose we walk into the sheriff? He thinks Roy is Patmore now. Who do we say I am?"

"Suppose we don't walk into him?" she said.

"I'm not in the position to take chances, and you know it."

"So what? Are you going to be scared from now on of ever going into Wentworth because you might just possibly run into that fat old fool?"

"If he gets an idea there is something wrong out here," I said, trying to keep my voice down, "he'll come out here and take a look around. He might even dig Jenson up. You wouldn't be quite so calm if he did that, would you? After all, you shot him."

"Did I? How does he prove that?"

I stared at her for a long moment, a little shocked and very uneasy.

"All right, let's drop it," I said. "We're in this jam together, Lola. I can't go to Wentworth tonight. I'm not taking any risks even if you want to."

She turned her back on me, shrugging.

"All right, so you're not going to Wentworth," she said. "It's not stopping me."

I went over to her and put my arms around her, pulling her against me.

"Don't be angry, sweetheart," I said. "You've got to realise . . ."

She jerked free of me.

"I'm busy. Can't you see? Haven't you anything to do?"

"Okay, if that's the way you feel about it."

She looked over her shoulder at me. Her green eyes were suddenly as hard as stone.

"That is the way I feel about it, and you'd better move in with your boy friend. I want the bungalow to myself."

"Now, look, Lola . . ."

"You heard what I said. You may not realise it but I own this place now. You two are such buddies. Well, go sleep with him!"

The sudden hatred in her eyes chilled me.

"Well, if that's the way you want it . . ."

"Oh, get out! I want a man in my bed, not a gutless insect. Go and talk to your boy friend!"

I went out, shutting the door behind me.

II

That was the end of my intimacy with Lola.

Funnily enough, now that Roy was here, I didn't mind. For

127

weeks now this business of going to the bungalow with her after we had locked up each night had given me a squeasy feeling. Every time I went into the big bedroom I thought of Jenson. I forgot about him as soon as I had Lola in my arms, but there was always this moment when I entered the room when I did think of him.

Roy helped me move the single bed into the cabin.

"So you're in the dog house," he said, grinning. "Women! They hold their sex over you like a club. I've had all I want of it. I'm beginning to see why Jenson walked out."

All day Lola had sulked, not speaking to me. Around ten o'clock she had got in the Mercury and had driven off to Wentworth. It was when she had gone that I moved my things out of the bungalow.

"She'll get over it," I said. "Anyway, it'll be a change to have some male company."

While he was servicing a car that had come in, I packed my things in a suitcase. I had put the .45 in the top drawer of the chest which I shared with Lola. When I came to look for it, it had gone.

This really rattled me. Only Lola could have taken it. I searched the drawers in the chest, but I didn't expect to find it and I didn't. I searched the whole room and the other rooms in the bungalow, but I didn't find it.

Why had she taken it?

The rest of the evening was spoilt for me. I kept worrying and thinking about the gun. I remembered that hard look of hatred that had come into her eyes.

I kept asking myself if our association together during the past weeks had been an act on her side.

I stayed up with Roy during his night shift, and we both turned in around one o'clock. I heard her come in around three o'clock. I was in bed by the window and I looked out, seeing her park the Mercury, and in the moonlight I watched her enter the bungalow. I was tempted to get out of bed and go over there and ask her about the gun, but I decided to wait until the morning. I didn't sleep much that night.

She didn't come into the lunch room until after eleven. Roy was peeling potatoes and I was washing the dishes from last night's trade.

She had a sulky expression on her face, but she greeted Roy well enough: me, she ignored.

Roy winked at me and jerked his head at the door. Then switching off the potato peeling machine, he went out, leaving us alone together.

"Where's the gun?" I said.

She stared at me.

"I got rid of it."

"How?"

"I buried it on the road to Wentworth. Does that satisfy you?"

I didn't know if she was lying or not.

"What's the idea then?"

"They could prove the gun shot him, couldn't they? It's safer to get rid of it."

That made sense, but I still wasn't sure if she had really got rid of it.

"And Chet, I've been thinking . . ."

"Well, go on. What have you been thinking?"

"Now you have your boy friend with you, you can run this place on your own. I'm leaving."

"Do you think that is a good idea?"

"Of course. I've always want to leave. I've told you that over and over again. Now with Roy here it is possible."

"What will the sheriff think when he finds you gone?"

"You can tell him I've gone to join Carl, and you two are in charge."

"You're forgetting every police station has my description and photograph. Sorry, Lola, that cat won't jump."

Her eyes began to glitter.

"You're going to open that safe, Chet, and you are giving me the money! I'm leaving at the end of the week! Do you understand?"

"It won't work, Lola, for three very solid reasons. First, I have to keep out of sight. If you leave, it will appear that Roy is running this place on his own and the Sheriff could get nosy enough to check up. If he finds me here, I'm sunk. Secondly, Jenson is buried here and if the police ever dig him up, you're going to be here to take the rap. You shot him, and it's your pigeon. Thirdly, I'm not opening the safe and you're not getting the money, for the moment you get it, I'll be in trouble. There'll be nothing to stop you from telling the police I killed Jenson, and that's something I'll take damn good care you don't tell them."

I expected her to fly into a rage, but she didn't. Her face lost some of its colour. Her eyes went dark, but otherwise she kept calm.

"Sure about it, Chet?"

"Yes."

"Just so long as I know. I've waited four years now to get away from this hell hole. I've learned to be patient. I'll get out of it and when I do, you'll be sorry I didn't leave sooner."

"If we are going to warn each other, Lola, let me warn you too. Roy could open that safe, but don't get that idea in your head. If he opened the safe and saw what was in it, he'd take it. I'm telling you. Don't kid yourself he would fall for you. I wouldn't have had him here if I thought for one moment you could make an impression on him. I've known him all my life. Women bounce off him. You've tried to make an impression on him already. It didn't work, did it? The only thing in life that means anything to him is money. He would take the money and ditch you. You would never touch it. Don't kid yourself. If you want to lose that money, ask him to open the safe."

I left her staring at me with narrowed eyes. I joined Roy who was sweeping up around the gas pumps.

He grinned at me.

"I thought I'd leave you two together. Have you kissed and made it up?"

"Not yet," I said. I couldn't help staring at him, wondering about him, asking myself if I could trust him not to make a fool of himself over Lola. Looking at his dark, cynical face, I tried to assure myself I could trust him. "She'll get over it."

"Treat them rough, Chet," he said. "No woman is worth a guy worrying himself. I found that out years ago. Relax. Don't look so worried. If she doesn't toe the line, there are plenty who will."

"Yeah, that's right. I have an idea, Roy, she's going to make a play at you to fix me. I just mention it. It's just an idea I have."

He laughed.

"That's funny. Okay, let her try. You know me, pal. She won't cut any ice with me. What's the idea then? Trying to make you jealous?"

I wondered if I should tell him about the safe, but I decided against it. If Roy knew there was all that money in the safe it would unsettle him. He would put pressure on me to try to persuade me to open the safe and that was something I wasn't going to do.

"That's the idea I guess."

He shook his head.

"Women!"

The next three days and nights must have been pretty lonely for Lola. As she continued to sulk with me, she found herself without anyone to talk to.

Roy and I kept together. We shared the night duty and we started a non-stop game of Gin. As soon as the traffic dropped off, we put a table on the veranda and started this game. We betted against each other on paper: no money passed between us, but we kept account.

Roy had a lot of luck, and he was a better player than I was. It was on the fourth night that he said with a grin, "You're in the hole for five hundred bucks. You should quit before I ruin you."

"You don't have to worry about ruining me," I said, grinning at him. "What you've got to worry about is when you're going to get paid."

"Piker!" He shuffled the cards. "I could do with five hundred bucks. Next week, the races start. There's a horse that's going to walk it. If I could put five hundred bucks on that gee, I'd clear five thousand." He whistled. "That's the kind of money I'd like to put my hands on."

I thought of the hundred thousand in the safe.

"You wouldn't know what to do with it if you had it," I said. "Come on: concentrate, or you'll be owing me money soon."

He sat back in his chair.

"I'd know what to do with it," he said. "With five thousand bucks I could buy myself a partnership in a wire service. I know a guy who wants a little extra capital. With three times that money I could buy him out, then Boy! would I be in the dough!"

"You're nuts. Who ever heard of anyone making money out of a wire service?"

"I'm serious, Chet. If I could get some capital together, I would really be in the money. Okay, five thousand wouldn't get me far, but fifty thousand would."

I shifted uneasily in my chair.

"Forget it! How could you ever scrape up fifty thousand?"

"We could do it in six months, Chet." He leaned forward to stare at me. "I've got it all worked out. Now look, at the back of here there's a couple of acres of good, solid sand. You could land a hoverplane there. I know a guy in Mexico who would pay a hundred dollars a head to land Mexican wetbacks here. We could ferry them into Wentworth and Tropica Springs and lose them there. This is the idea place for a racket like that."

"I told you I was through with rackets, and I mean it. If you're not happy here, Roy, say so. I want you here, but if you want to start that kind of thing, you'll have to start it some place else."

Roy began to deal the cards.

"Well, okay," he said, but this time he didn't look at me. "I think you're passing up a good thing, but this is your show and not mine. I've got to get me some money before long. I've got to get some big money. I'd hate to break this up, but I'll have to in a while. I'll stick around for a bit, but I can't afford to stay here indefinitely. I've got to dream up a way to get some money."

"Don't be a fool, Roy," I said sharply. "You are heading for trouble the way you're thinking. Here, you are on your own, you are your own boss and can live damn well. This money itch is no good. If you had been to Farnworth . . ."

"I know, but it so happens, Chet, I haven't been to Farnworth, and you wouldn't have been there if you had done what I had told you to instead of rushing down to the street."

131

"Oh, forget it!" I said. "Let's play if we're going to play."

We played a couple of hands and I won them both. Roy wasn't concentrating. I knew he was still thinking about this pipe dream of his. Suddenly he dropped his cards on the table.

"Let's chuck it," he said. "I'm tired. I guess I'll hit the sack."

It was my turn for night duty. This was the first time in five days that Roy wasn't sharing it with me.

"Sure, go ahead," I said.

He got up and stretched elaborately, yawning.

"See you in the morning. So long."

I watched him walk over to the cabin. I watched the light go up in the window. Across the way, Lola's light was still on.

I looked from one light to the other.

I had an idea that Roy was suddenly hostile to me.

That made two of them.

CHAPTER TWELVE

I

BUT I needn't have worried.

The next morning, Roy was his old self again. I realised he had been disappointed that I had turned down his Mexican emigrant idea, but having slept on it, he seemed to have put it out of his mind.

We played Gin in the evening and we kidded each other about his winnings, and we talked about this and that, but we didn't talk about hoverplanes nor about quick, easy money.

I was relieved, not only because he was back in form, but also because Lola was slowly thawing out. She had spoken to me once or twice during the day: strictly business, but at least she was speaking.

Around ten o'clock that evening, she came out on the veranda and watch us playing Gin.

"Why not join us?" I said. "I'll get another chair."

"Cards are a waste of time," she said. "I'm going to bed. I have to be up early. I have a lot of stuff to get from Wentworth tomorrow. Which of you is coming to give me a hand?"

Up to now, she had always managed on her own when marketing in Wentworth. Her request startled me. While I was hesitating, Roy said, "If you don't want to go, Chet, I'd be glad to. I haven't been off the place since I've been here. There are things I want to buy. Okay?"

I felt a sudden stab of suspicion. I looked at him. He was lighting a cigarette and his face, lit by the flame of the lighter, was casual.

"Why, sure," I said. "You'll be back by lunch time. I can manage until then."

"I'll be leaving at eight," Lola said. "Good night," and she walked away towards the bungalow.

"I've got to get me some shirts and a pair of shoes," Roy said as he picked up his cards.

My suspicions died down. It was true he hadn't left Point of No Return since he had been here. It was reasonable that he should want some new clothes, but I wished he wasn't going with Lola. That bothered me. I was sure she would get to work on him. A twenty mile drive into Wentworth and back was too long for them to be alone together.

"Relax, pea brain," Roy said and reaching out, he slapped me on the knee. "I know what you're thinking—let her try. She'll cut no ice with me."

"I'm not worrying," I said.

But when I saw them go off together the following morning, I felt lonely and uneasy. To get my mind off them, I began to take down the engine of the Station wagon, but even working on a job I liked, I kept thinking and wondering and worrying.

A big truck, loaded with wooden crates, pulled up by the gas pumps. The driver was a thickset, elderly man. His blond hair was shot with white and his red, heavy face was shaded by a Stetson hat.

While I was filling the tanks, he climbed down from the cab, wiping his face with a grimy handkerchief.

"You're new around here, aren't you?" he said, looking curiously at me. "Where's Carl Jenson?"

I spotted he was a Swede, and that warned me he might be a friend of Jenson's. I gave him the story that Jenson was in Arizona.

For some reason this seemed to bother him. I saw his face tighten and his staring eyes harden.

"I've never known him to leave here before," he said. "I've been through here off and on for the past twenty years, and I've always found him here. Arizona, huh? Going to open a new gas station? Does that mean he isn't coming back?"

"He'll be back to clear up."

"Did he take his wife with him?"

"She's running this place while he's away. I'm just helping out."

"Are you a friend of hers?" he asked as I screwed on the caps to the tanks.

"I'm just hired to help out. What do you mean?"

"She's no good. You could have knocked me over with a puff of wind when I found her here, married to Jenson." He leaned up against the side of the truck and began to roll a cigarette. "I knew her in Carson City. That was five years ago. Then she was married to a guy named Frank Finney. He ran a repair station and a snack bar: she helped out. It wasn't his place: he just ran it. Know what happened to him?"

I was listening, tense, not missing a word.

"They found him dead in the snack bar one morning. There was a gun in his hand and his brains all over the floor. Her story was she heard the shot when she was upstairs. She came down and found him. There was a check on the till. They found over two thousand bucks missing. It looked like Finney had been robbing the till for months. They never found the money. The cops reckoned she had it, but they never proved it. There was one cop who even figured she shot Finney. They had been quarrelling for months, but they never proved that either. She left town soon after. Imagine my surprise to find her here, married to a good man like Jenson."

"First time I've heard of it," I said, managing to keep my face expressionless.

"It's not the kind of thing she would advertise," the trucker said. "Jenson is okay, isn't he? He really is in Arizona?"

I suddenly felt cold. This was dangerous. This Swede could be a lot more dangerous than Ricks.

"He's fine," I said, forcing myself to meet the pale, staring eyes. "I had a letter from him the other day. He's pretty pleased with this new filling station. Maybe the next time you come through you'll catch him."

He looked relieved.

"I'm damn glad to hear it. You know, for a moment, when you said he wasn't here, it jumped into my mind that—well, I thought maybe he was dead."

I was really sweating now.

"This story about her shooting her husband," I said, "there was no proof, was there?"

He suddenly looked embarrassed.

"No, but there was a lot of talk."

"As far as I can see, Mrs. Jenson makes Mr. Jenson very happy," I said. "He wouldn't like a story like that going around. I reckon he'd be pretty angry with you if he heard what you've been saying."

"You mean he's really happy with her?"

"That's what I'm telling you."

"Well . . . yeah, maybe, I have shot my mouth off. You forget it, will you? Don't mention it to Mr. Jenson."

"You forget it too." I took his money. "That kind of talk can cause an awful lot of mischief."

He got in the cab, slammed the door and drove off. I could see from the expression on his face I had thrown a scare into him.

He had certainly thrown a scare into me.

I stood staring after him.

Thoughts raced through my mind. So Lola had been married before. Her husband had died violently, and there had been money missing. I felt a tightening in my chest. Jenson had also died violently, and maybe, if I hadn't slammed the door of the safe shut, more money would have been missing.

I walked over to the lunch room veranda and sat down. I lit a cigarette, aware my hands were shaking.

My mind was now buzzing with alarm and suspicion.

According to the trucker, the Carson City police had thought Lola had not only taken the money, but she had murdered her husband.

Had she murdered Jenson?

I thought back on that scene that now seemed terribly near to me and startlingly vivid. In my mind, I say her come into the sitting-room. I could almost hear her quick, hard breathing. She had the gun in her hand. I heard again the fast, unreal dialogue. I remembered Jenson, red in the face with anger, getting to his feet.

I saw Lola looking at me as I slammed the safe door shut, then I heard again the bang of the gun.

I had been convinced then that the sound of the safe door shutting had made her accidentally tighten her finger on the gun trigger. The gun had gone off, and Jenson had been killed.

Accidentally?

I threw the half smoked cigarette away and wiped my face with the back of my hand.

Accidentally was now the operative word.

She was suspected of murdering her first husband and money was missing. Had the shooting of Jenson been deliberate?

It had looked like an accident, but had it been, after all, murder? She could have pinned the murder on me. Then I had another idea that made my heart skip a beat.

The safe door had been open when she had come into the room with the gun. Suppose she had planned first to shoot Jenson, and then me, and then take the money from the safe? Suppose this had been her plan? She could have hidden the money and then called the police. Her story would be that she and Jenson had caught me opening the safe. I had murdered Jenson. By some trick, she had got the gun from me and had shot me in self defence. I was an escapee from Farnworth: a man with a reputation. That fat sheriff from Wentworth might very easily have accepted such a story.

But she hadn't killed me because I had shut the safe as she had shot Jenson. She had been quick enough and smart enough to know that she couldn't open the safe, but that I could. When she found she couldn't blackmail me into opening it, she had had this sudden change of heart and had pretended to be in love with me. She had suddenly turned hostile when she had discovered I now wasn't the only one at Point of No Return who could open the safe! Roy could open it!

She had the gun. I was now sure her story of getting rid of it had been a lie.

That could mean both Roy's life and mine were in danger. She could persuade Roy to open the safe, then she would kill him. She could kill me too. Her story could be more or less the same as the one she would have told if she had killed me when she had shot Jenson.

I got to my feet.

This was guess work, sparked off by the mischievous talk of an old Swedish trucker. The chances were that this guy Finney had committed suicide and Jenson's shooting had been an accident, but I wasn't going to take chances. I remembered those hard green eyes. There was one way to fix her. I would take the money from the safe, leaving the safe door open so she would know that there was no point in working on Roy or planning to murder me.

I had to find a safe hiding place for the money, but that wouldn't be difficult. I looked at my wrist watch. The time was ten minutes past ten. They wouldn't be back until mid-day. I would bury the money in Jenson's grave. If she wanted it, she would have to dig him up as well.

It was a good idea, but it didn't work out.

As I started over to the bungalow, a truck, towing a 1955 Packard came down the Wentworth road and I had a major repair job on my hands.

The driver of the Packard was in a hurry to get to Tropica Springs. He was an aggressive and impatient salesman. He wouldn't take no for an answer.

I was still working on the Packard when Lola and Roy came back from Wentworth.

II

For the next three days and nights I never had a chance of getting near the safe.

Lola was always around. She had given up night work, and as soon as Roy and I settled down to our game of Gin, she went to bed.

She was now on speaking terms with me, but there was a reserve in her manner that warned me we could no longer be on the same terms as we had been before Roy arrived. I made no attempt to touch her. I didn't even want to touch her. I was suspicious of her, watching her all the time for some sign that might confirm that she was planning to murder me, but the sign wasn't there.

I also watched Roy, anxious to see if there was now any change in his attitude after his drive with her to Wentworth, but, here again, I saw no change.

There were moments when I was tempted to take him into my confidence, but I didn't. I had an instinctive feeling that the the knowledge that what was in that safe would be too much for the urge in him to lay his hands on any easy money. So I held back, hoping sooner or later, she and he would go into Wentworth again, and I could get at the safe.

The chance came about a week later when Lola said as we were clearing up after a busy supper trade, "There's a good movie on in Wentworth. I want to see it. This French star: Brigitte Bardot. I want to see her. Is anyone coming?"

Roy shook his head.

"Not me—I only go for gangster pictures."

Here was the chance I was looking for. They wouldn't be back before three o'clock in the morning. I would have all the time I wanted to get the money from the safe and bury it before they returned. After midnight, I wouldn't have to worry about any interruptions.

"I'm stuck here, Roy," I said. "I can't go into Wentworth. It's my turn for night duty anyway. Take a chance: you might get a kick out of a French star."

He looked at me, puzzled.

"I'd just as soon play cards."

"Pretty tough on Lola to go twenty miles on her own."

I was scared I was overplaying my hand for now Lola was staring at me, but this was a chance I had to take.

"Well, when you two have made up your minds," she said. "You don't have to do me a favour. I can go on my own."

Roy suddenly grinned.

"Okay: you have a date," he said. "Let's go."

Soon after half past nine, Lola came from the bungalow. She was wearing a white frock I hadn't seen before. It was tight across her chest and flared out over her hips. She had taken a lot of trouble with her make-up. The sight of her set my heart thumping which irritated me.

I watched her get in the Mercury beside Roy. He grinned at me as he gunned the engine.

Out of the corner of his mouth, he said, "This was your idea, pal: not mine."

It was a remark I hadn't expected from him, but I didn't care. Once I had the money buried, I had the whip hand over them both.

"Have a good time," I said.

Lola was staring at me. Her green eyes were mocking.

"We will. Don't let the place run away."

Roy shifted from neutral into drive, and the Mercury moved off.

For some moments I stood motionless, watching the red tail lights climbing the hill towards Wentworth, then I started for the bungalow, but I might have known it wasn't going to be that easy.

The bungalow door was locked. The lock wasn't anything, but I had to go to the repair shed for a length of wire. I then had to fashion the wire into a pick, and it took me a few moments to get the lock turned.

I went into the sitting-room and squatted down before the safe. Opening it was nothing. I had done it often enough, but this night, probably because I was nervous, I took longer than I had done before. Then just as I was opening the safe door, I heard the honk of a car horn.

A grey and yellow Cadillac stood by the pumps.

I spun the dial, making sure the door was locked again, then cursing to myself, I went out and fed gas into the car.

The driver, his wife and four awful kids wanted food. I fixed them sandwiches. They were in the lunch room for thirty minutes. As they drove away, a truck came in and the trucker wanted ham and eggs.

So it went on.

I expected this, and it didn't worry me. This was routine. Around midnight, the traffic would stop. I would still have three hours in which to do the job—it was enough.

At midnight the traffic did stop. I sat on the veranda, watching the long, winding road, lit by the moon for ten minutes before I got to my feet and started towards the bungalow again. Then I paused, and this time I felt a nudge of desperation as I saw the headlights of a fast approaching car.

I was pretty certain the car would stop, at least for gas. I walked to the pumps to save time.

As the car pulled up, I saw it was an old, dusty Buick. There were two men in it. The driver leaned out of the window, looking towards me.

He was a man around my own age, wearing a black slouch hat, a black shirt and a white tie. His sun-tanned face was thin and hatchet shaped. His small dark eyes were like bits of glass, and as expressionless.

His companion was fat, oily and swarthy with a straggly moustache and the narrow, olive black eyes of a Mexican. He was wearing a shabby, stained light grey suit and a Mexican hat, the cord under his fat chin.

There was something about these two I didn't like. I had an instinctive feeling they were dangerous. This was the first time since I had been at Point of No Return that I was suddenly conscious that I was alone, and this was a lonely spot.

The Mexican was eyeing me over while the other man was looking around, his hard, bleak eyes probing the shadows.

"Shall I fill her up?" I said, unhooking the gas hose.

"Yeah: fill her up," the Mexican said.

The man in the white tie moved from the car, still looking around. As I switched on the pump and began to shoot gas into the car, I watched him. He took off his hat and began to fan himself with it. His thinning, black hair was wet with sweat.

"It sure is hot," I said. "One of the hottest nights I've known."

I was talking for the sake of talking. These two bothered me. I had an idea they might knock me on the head and rifle the till. Then a thought came into my mind that sent a chill through my blood. Suppose they found the safe in the bungalow . . . !

The man in the white tie had taken a pin from his coat lapel. He began to pick his teeth. I was aware now that he was staring at me: not at my face, but at the V opening of my open neck shirt.

"Is this your joint, bright boy?" he asked abruptly. He had a soft, drawling voice. "Have you a wife and kids here?"

It was the kind of question anyone could ask, but somehow, coming from him, there was something sinister about it.

"I'm just the hired hand," I said, watching the dial spin on the pump. "My boss and the other hired hand will be in at any minute now."

I figured it might be an idea to let them know I wasn't going to be alone much longer.

He dug into his teeth with the ping, then sucked it and put it back into his lapel.

I switched off the pump, then picked the sponge out of the bucket and began to wipe over the windshield. I was watching these two the way you would watch a snake that has crawled into the bathroom while you are taking a tub.

"Let's have something to eat, Sol," the man in the white tie said to the Mexican. He looked at me. "What have you got, bright boy?"

"At this hour, there's only sandwiches," I said.

"It had better be better than sandwiches. Come on, shake the ants out of your pants. I'm hungry."

I sneaked a look at my wrist watch. The time was twenty minutes past midnight. Lola and Roy wouldn't be back yet for at least two and a half hours. It looked as if I were stuck with these two.

I walked to the lunch room. The two men sauntered after me. They paused just inside the room, looking around.

"Anyone else here?" the man in the white tie asked.

He could easily find out for himself, so I said there was no one else here.

"Let's eat: what have you got?"

"You can have fried chicken if you want to wait or there's hamburgers and sandwiches."

Sol walked past me, around the counter, pushed open the kitchen door and looked inside. He came back, shaking his head at the man in the white tie.

Then I knew I was in for trouble.

The man in the white tie said, "This your only phone?" He tapped the telephone on the wall.

"Yes," I said. I kept my hands on my hips. I was very careful not to make any hurried movements.

He took hold of the telephone receiver and jerked the wire away from its moorings. As he did so, his snake's eyes watched me.

"Get that chicken cooking. You watch him, Sol."

I went into the kitchen with Sol, breathing heavily, on my heels.

"What's the idea?" I said as I started to heat up the chicken.

"Just relax, Pal," Sol said, sitting on the table. His fat, brown hand caressed his gun butt. "Never mind with the questions."

There was a pause, then he said, "Do you like it here, pal? Don't you find it lonely?"

"I'm used to it," I said, aware my lips felt stiff and my heart was thumping.

"You married?"

"No."

"How do you get on for a woman, then?"

"I manage."

The man in the white tie came in, carrying a plate of sandwiches he had taken from the glass case in the lunch room.

"Help yourself, Sol: these ain't so lousy." He was speaking with his mouth crammed full of food. "Watch the bright boy and keep him amused. I'm going to take a look around."

Sol picked up two of the sandwiches and began to eat. The man in the white tie went out.

"Eddy's a bright boy," Sol said to me. "You have to treat him gently. "He's got a trigger itch, but treated right, he's bright."

I didn't say anything. There was nothing to say, but I was doing a lot of thinking.

This fat Mexican didn't look so hard to take. If I could put him out of action, I was ready to take on Eddy: not the two of them, but one at the time didn't seem too hard.

Sol said, "How much dough have you got in this dump?"

"Not much," I said. "We banked this afternoon."

"Yeah? That's rough. We want dough: we want it bad." He scooped up two more sandwiches and began to cram them into his vast mouth. "We reckoned a dump like this would have plenty of dough stashed away somewhere."

"There's a hundred bucks in the till," I said.

"There'd better be a damn sight more than that, pal, or you might get a broken neck."

I put two plates on the table. I was breathing fast. If I was going to take this hunk of fat now was the time.

I picked up the frying pan, containing the chicken and the boiling fat.

"There's the gas money," I went on as I walked over to the table. "Maybe there's fifty bucks in the satchel, but not more."

He shifted his bulk off the table and stood watching me as, scoop in hand, I made ready to slide the chicken onto the plates.

"You'll have to find more, pal," he said. "Ed isn't the kind of guy you can stall."

With a flicking movement of my wrist I tossed the contents of the frying pan into his fat face.

The hot oil made his scream, and he staggered back. The chicken dripped down his coat: some of it lodged in his hat. His hand groped wildly for his gun as I slammed him across the face with the hot frying pan. Then as he reeled back, I jumped forward and belted him on the side of his jaw. He went down. Bending over him, I got his gun. I hit him on his forehead with the gun butt as he tried to struggle up. He flopped down and his eyes rolled back.

I had his gun.

As I straightened I heard the lunch room door creak open. I jumped across the room and turned off the light.

I didn't underestimate Eddy. He was a professional killer. But at least I had a gun.

CHAPTER THIRTEEN

I

"Sol . . .?"

The man in the white tie's voice was an alert whisper.

I took two silent steps sideways that brought me to the back door. I was no gunman. The heavy .45 felt awkward in my hand, but it gave me a lot of comfort.

The light went out in the lunch room. I heard a board creak. "You there, Sol?"

I put my hand on the door handle and gently eased the door open. I would stand a better chance, I told myself, in the open.

I heard Sol stir and then groan. He must have had a head like concrete. I had reckoned he would have remained out of action long enough for me to take care of Eddy, but it looked as if I would have to work fast or I would have the two of them after me.

The back door was open now. Only a couple of days before, I had oiled the hinges and it opened silently.

I felt the hot air from the desert strike my face as I edged backwards, holding the .45 stiffly, pointing at the kitchen door.

The bang and flash of a gun and the deadly zip of a slug that almost brushed my hair sent my heart racing and brought sweat pouring down my face.

I jumped down the three steps and crouched in the darkness. That kind of shooting was a little too good.

I waited, listening, but hearing only the thud-thud-thud of my heart beats. I looked quickly up the white road, picked out by the moonlight, but there were no headlights coming. I was alone. If I was going to get out of this jam, I would have to rely on myself.

There was a big patch of moonlight flooding the gas pumps. Around the lunch room and the repair shed there was heavy darkness. The bungalow was also in darkness, but to get there, I would have to cross the patch of moonlight.

Moving step by step, keeping just by the wall of the lunch room, I edged backwards.

A soft voice called out of the darkness: "Hey, bright boy,

drop the rod and come back here with your hands in the air. Come on! Drop the rod!"

That insinuating, confident voice nearly persuaded me to fire in its direction, but I just stopped in time. I realised the flash of my gun would pin point me. That was what he wanted. I would miss him, but I was pretty sure he wouldn't miss me.

Crouching in the darkness, I remained motionless, straining my eyes in the direction of the voice, but I couldn't see him.

"Come on, bright boy," the voice went on. "Drop the rod. You won't get hurt if you come with your hands in the air. I just want your dough. Come on."

Was the voice closer? It seemed to me it was

I was pretty scared. I knew if he caught sight of me, If he spotted where I was, he would kill me.

Very slowly, I eased myself to the ground. As I did so, my hand touched a stone. My fingers closed over it. I picked it up and tossed it into the darkness, away from me. It rattled against the wall of the lunch room on the other side of the steps.

The bang of the gun sounded violently loud and the flash was blinding. A slug zipped over my head. If I hadn't been flat on the ground, he would have nailed me. He hadn't shot away from me: he had shot at me, and that showed if nothing else could, just how professional he was.

The flash came from the top of the steps, but from the sudden flurry of sound, I knew he had jumped off the steps and was crouching behind them, facing me.

I began to edge backwards, expecting any moment to hear another bang from his gun and feel a slug rip into me.

Then I saw him.

Something white moved about fifteen yards from me. That could only be his white tie. For a professional gunman, he wasn't too smart to wear a white tie: a target, even a sucker like me couldn't very well miss.

Very cautiously, I lifted the gun and sighted it on that white blur. My finger began to take up the slack on the trigger, then a thought dropped into my mind. Suppose I killed him? What then?

In a moment of emergency like this, it's surprising how fast the mind can work. If I killed him, I would have his body on my hands. What about the Mexican? What would I do with him? Suppose I had to kill him too?

I couldn't call the police and report an attempted robbery nor tell them I had shot these two. Roy couldn't substitute for me again. The M.O. might be old fashioned, but not old fashioned enough not to know these two men had died while Roy and Lola were on their way back from Wentworth. The police would want to know who had killed them. If they found out I had killed them, there would be Farnworth waiting for me.

Hesitating, I lowered the gun. That was a mistake.

The slight movement must have caught Eddy's eyes.

I felt a numbing blow in my chest as, at the same time, I heard the bang of his gun and saw the flash.

I didn't feel any pain.

It was as if someone had turned off a switch inside me, cutting off my strength the way you cut off an electric light.

I felt the hot sand against my face, and although I made an effort to keep a grip on the gun, it suddenly became impossibly heavy. I felt it slip away from me as a hard pointed shoe thudded into my ribs.

That kick released a white hot pain inside my chest. I was suddenly going down into the scorching mouth of a volcano. I tried to yell for help, but no sound came out of my throat, only a sudden rushing of hot blood that threatened to drown me.

The clock was spinning backwards.

I was running blindly down the stairs that led away from Henry Cooper's luxury penthouse. I was wrestling again with the doorman, then I was in the street, hearing the thud of feet as the cop chased me. I heard again the bang of his gun and the tearing, blinding pain in my chest.

Roy told me later he had found me lying by the kitchen door. Both he and Lola had known something was wrong as there were no lights showing.

Roy had gone around, shouting for me. It took him some minutes to find me, and when he did, he thought I was dead.

Between them, Lola and he carried me into the cabin and got me on the bed. It was while Roy was cutting away my shirt that I came to.

I found him bending over me, his face white, his hands shaking.

I looked beyond him, and there was Lola standing behind him, as white and as tense as he was.

I felt pretty bad, and it was an effort even to shift my head.

"What happened?" Lola demanded, coming around Roy and bending over me. "Who did it?"

I tried to speak, but the words wouldn't come.

Roy said, "Leave him alone. Let me fix him."

I was drifting away again into darkness. I wondered if I was dying: the thought didn't worry me. It was with a sense of relief that as I lost consciousness, the pain went away.

The sun was shining through the window when I became conscious again.

Roy was still there, sitting by the bed, watching me, but Lola had gone.

"How do you feel?" Roy asked, leaning forward.

"Okay."

The word was an effort to get out. I felt curiously weak, and there was an odd floating sensation inside me.

"Look, Chet," Roy spoke slowly, pronouncing each word clearly as if he were talking to a foreigner, "you're pretty ill. I want to get a doctor to look at you, but Lola won't let me. She said you wouldn't want a doctor."

"I don't want one."

"You'd better have a doctor, Chet." His face was anxious. "You're pretty bad. I've done what I can for you, but it's not enough."

Bad as I felt, my brain wasn't paralysed. A doctor would have to report to the police when he found I had been shot: then Farnworth.

Through the open window came the sound of the impatient honking of a horn.

Muttering, Roy got to his feet.

"These truckers are driving me nuts. I'll be back."

I closed my eyes and dozed off.

The sun had shifted to the back of the lunch room when a movement close to me brought me awake.

Lola was bending over me.

"Who was it who shot you?"

"Two gunmen," I said. She had to bend close to hear me. "I've never seen them before."

"Did they open the safe?"

I looked at her. I scarcely recognised her. There was a scraped, bony look on her face that made her seem ten years older. I could see tiny sweat beads along her upper lip. Her face was chalk white.

"I don't know."

And lying there, feeling this odd floating sensation inside me, I didn't care.

"Did they mention the safe?" Her voice was shaking.

"No."

"It's shut. It doesn't look as if they tampered with it." I could see her breasts under her overall rising and falling in her agitation. "I must know! Suppose they've taken the money! I must know if it has gone!"

I thought of Eddy. He was a professional. If he had found the safe, he would have opened it. Anyone with the slightest knowledge of safes could open that sardine can.

"They could have taken it," I said.

146

This effort at talking was making me feel bad. I began to float away into darkness again.

"I must know! Tell me how to open the safe!"

Her white tense face hung over me. I could smell the sweat of fear from her. I could feel the frustrated greed coming out of her like the sound waves from a radio set.

The darkness closed up around me.

From a long way off, I heard her saying, "I must know! Pull yourself together! Tell me how to open it!"

The voice, the room and the sunshine coming through the window were suddenly no longer there.

II

For the next three days I hung between life and death. I knew it, and I didn't care.

I wouldn't have lasted a day if it hadn't been for Roy. He scarcely left my side, and when I developed a fever, he sat over me with an ice bag and kept right by me until the fever broke.

There was a time, when the fever was at its height, that, as I lay burning and in pain, I suddenly saw Carl Jenson in the room.

He had the same bewildered expression on his face that I had seen when he had caught me before the open safe. I tried to speak to him, but the words didn't come. After a while, he went away. I didn't see him again. That was when I nearly died. Later, Roy told me he had given me up, then the fever broke and I began to get better.

It wasn't until the seventh day that I was able to talk about Eddy and the Mexican.

"They cleared out the till," Roy told me, "and they took the gas money and most of the food."

I wondered about the safe. I wondered if Eddy had found it and had opened it, but I didn't mention it to Roy.

"It seems to me you're going to pull out of this now," he went on. He looked thin and tired, and there were dark smudges under his eyes that told of loss of sleep. "It was a near thing. You are lucky."

"You saved my life, Roy," I said. "Well, that makes the score even. Thanks."

"What did you expect me to do—let you croak?" He grinned. "It's been pretty rugged, keeping the place going and nursing you, but now I reckon I can catch up on some sleep."

I had been out of action for eight days and nights. During

that time, Lola hadn't been near me. I wondered if she had made any headway with Roy during that time.

"How are you and Lola making out?" I asked.

He shrugged.

"I scarcely see her. I've been too busy looking after you." It was too glib, he didn't look at me. I knew he was lying.

"I've warned you, Roy. She's dangerous."

"She isn't cutting any ice with me, and she never will," he said. There was a long pause while we looked at each other. Then abruptly he asked, "What really happened to Jenson?"

I wouldn't have told him unless I was sure she had made an impression on him. I was desperate enough to try to scare him off her by telling him the truth.

"She murdered him, and I was fool enough to bury him."

I saw his eyes go suddenly blank the way they always went when he heard something he didn't want to hear.

"She murdered her first husband too," I went on. "She's a killer, Roy, so watch out."

"Do you realise what you are saying?" he asked, leaning forward, his face tight and hard.

"I know what I'm saying: I'm warning you."

He stood up.

"I don't want to hear any more of this. Can't you see it puts me on a spot?"

"You've got to be warned, Roy. You don't know her the way I know her."

He moved to the door.

"I guess I'd better get back to work. I'll be in again. You take it easy."

Without looking at me, he went away.

Well, he knew now. He would be on his guard. She wouldn't fool him as easily as she had fooled Jenson and me.

But I didn't know I was already too late with my warning. I found that out the following night.

Roy had moved his bed into the sitting-room to give me more room.

He had told me if I wanted anything to call him, but if it wasn't urgent he would be glad to get some sleep. That was understandable. I said I would be all right and for him not to worry about me.

Since I had told him about Jenson's death, I knew it wasn't the same between us, and I knew it could never be the same with us again. It was in the atmosphere rather than in his attitude. He had always been poker-faced, and now he was even more so.

Neither of us mentioned Lola. From time to time I saw her

from the window, moving from the lunch room to the bungalow. She continued to keep away from me.

It was on the following night that I realised my warning had come too late.

Around midnight, Roy shut up the lunch room and turned off the light. I had seen Lola go to the bungalow a few minutes after eleven o'clock. The lights were out in the bungalow by the time Roy came into the cabin.

He opened my bedroom door silently and stood there, listening.

I had turned off my light some time ago. I made no sound.

"Are you awake, Chet?"

His whisper was so soft I scarcely heard it.

I stayed motionless, not saying anything. Then I heard the door shut softly.

I waited, hoping that what I knew was going to happen wouldn't happen, but of course it did.

For a few tense minutes I lay looking out of the window, then I saw Roy come out of the shadows. He walked quickly across to the bungalow, paused to look back at the cabin, then he opened the front door and went in.

I might have known he couldn't have resisted her for those eight days and nights when she could have worked on him un-interrupted.

I didn't blame him. I knew her technique. I had been kidding myself all along that Roy was indifferent to women, and Roy had been kidding himself too.

I felt helpless and pretty bad: jealousy didn't come into it, but fear did.

Once she had her claws in Roy, she would persuade him to open the safe. Then she would murder him. I was sure of that. I had warned her he wouldn't let her have the money once he got his hands on it. She would murder him, and then she would murder me. She would then hide the money and send for the fat sheriff. How she would explain what I was doing in pyjamas with a bullet wound in my chest I couldn't imagine, but she had had eight days to dream up a story and I was pretty sure, by now, she had one ready. I had given Roy a description of Eddy and the fat Mexican. He had certainly passed the descriptions on to Lola. She might even claim that these two had murdered Roy and me while she was in Wentworth. There were any number of angles she could use.

I lay there, enduring the nagging pain in my chest, while I watched the bungalow and schemed.

It was a little after two o'clock when I saw him come out. He closed the front door, then walked over to the cabin. He came in silently.

I reached for the light switch, and as he eased open my door I turned on the light.

He stood, startled, in the doorway, staring at me. He had on a singlet, a pair of trousers, and his feet were bare.

"I didn't mean to wake you," he said. "I just looked in to see if you were okay."

"Come in. I want to talk to you."

His eyes shifted.

"It's after two. I want to get some sleep."

"I want to talk to you."

He came in and sat down, away from me, and lit a cigarette. "What's on your mind?"

"She's thrown a hook into you, hasn't she?"

He blew a cloud of smoke that half screened his face, then he said, his voice harsh, "You're pretty sick, Chet. You don't want to work yourself up. Suppose we talk about this tomorrow? You need your sleep—so do I."

"I may be sick, but if you don't watch out, you're going to be a damn sight more than sick—you're going to be dead. You didn't answer my question."

"No woman will ever hook me," he said, his face now dead-pan.

"Are you trying to kid me or yourself?"

He didn't like that.

"Okay, if you must know, I took what she threw at me, but there are no strings to it—I'll take care of that."

"Did she ask you to open the safe?"

His eyes narrowed.

"Safe? What safe?"

"Jenson's safe."

He ran his fingers through his hair as he stared at me.

"What about Jenson's safe?"

"Did she ask you to open it?"

I saw by the puzzled expression on his face that she hadn't. I began to breathe more freely. At least, this time, I wasn't going to be too late to warn him.

"She's never mentioned a safe."

"She will, and she will ask you to open it."

He made an exasperated movement with his hands.

"What the hell is this about? What are you getting at?"

"There's something in that safe she wants," I said, "and when she wants something as badly as she wants this thing in the safe she will stop at nothing to get it, and I mean nothing. She shot her husband to get it. She tried to blackmail me into getting it, and now you arrive. Someone else who can open the safe, and she's starting to soften you up so if you open it she can take you by surprise and murder you. It sounds fantastic, doesn't it? It isn't! She'll murder you as she murdered her first husband, as she murdered Jenson and very nearly murdered me. I'm telling you—don't open that safe!"

By now the effort of talking had taken so much out of me I was sweating, and the pain in my chest was making me short of breath. I watched him in despair, for there was no change of expression, just the dead-pan look, and the eyes that had gone a shade darker.

"You sound crazy in the head," he said. "What is it she wants so badly?"

I wasn't going to tell him it was over a hundred thousand dollars in hard cash. I wasn't that much of a fool.

"I told you the cops suspected she had murdered her first husband," I said. "She did murder him. Before he married her, Jenson made her sign a confession and it is in the safe. I've seen it. Until the safe is open and she can destroy the confession, she's jail bait, and she knows it."

He rubbed the back of his neck, frowning.

"Are you dreaming all this or is it true?"

"She shot Jenson and she would have shot me only I got the safe door shut before she could pull the trigger. She knew I was the only one here who could open the safe and that saved my life. Now she has you in her sights. Don't open that safe, Roy."

"This doesn't add up," he said. "If she was going to murder you, how come you went to bed with her?"

I was ready for that one. It was the obvious question he was bound to ask.

"She couldn't do a thing to me so long as that safe remained shut. We lived here together and alone for five weeks before I touched her. I did it only because, like with you, she threw herself at me. She came into this room one night, and that was it."

I felt cold sweat on my face now and I was having trouble in breathing.

Roy, seeing the state I was in, came over to me.

"Hey! You've got to quiet down. Don't you understand how bad you are? Quit getting yourself excited—relax!"

I caught hold of his wrist.

"If you open that safe, Roy, she'll kill both of us! I'm warning you! If you open that safe we're both sunk!"

"Take it easy, fella. She hasn't even asked me to open the safe."

I had shot my bolt. I dropped back on the pillow. I couldn't make any more effort. I had warned him. I could only hope I had beaten her this time.

He stayed with me until I had drifted off into a heavy sleep.

When I woke the next morning the clock by the bed told me it was twenty to ten. I had had a long sleep and I felt better, a little stronger, but not strong enough to get up.

Later, Roy came in and shaved me. He was quiet, and neither of us mentioned the safe, but I knew it was big in both our minds.

The day dragged by. I was content to lie by the window and watch the activity going on outside. Both Lola and Roy slaved. The lunch room was busy during the lunch hour and again at night.

Finally, around ten o'clock, the traffic died away and Roy found time to bring me a bowl of soup.

"It's been some day," he said, leaning against the wall. "I'll be glad when you are up and about again."

"I'll be about," I said.

"Yeah." He stroked his nose, his black eyes watching me. "While we were having supper, she asked me if I could open a Lawrence safe."

I slopped a little of the soup.

"She did?"

"Yeah. I said I couldn't say until I had seen it."

My heart was thumping now.

"What did she say?"

"A trucker came in and broke it up. We didn't get around to it again."

"So long as that safe remains shut, you're okay and so am I. I'm not kidding, Roy."

"Okay, so you're not kidding. If it's all this bad, how about lending me Jenson's gun—the one he shot hawks with?"

"She's got it."

That jolted him. His eyes narrowed and his mouth tightened.

"She took it," I went on. "She told me she had got rid of it, but I know different."

"Well, she hasn't asked me to open the safe yet."

"She will." We left it like that.

Nothing happened for four days. According to Roy, Lola didn't mention the safe to him again. I made slow progress, but I still wasn't strong enough to get out of bed. I was more easy in my mind for Roy didn't go to the bungalow. At least, I seemed to have thrown a scare into him.

But on the fifth night, I woke around three o'clock in the morning and, looking out of the window, I saw a light on in the sitting-room of the bungalow. That gave me a hell of a jolt. I called out to Roy, but got no answer. He was over there with her and with the safe!

I was tempted to get out of bed and go over there, but I knew

I would never have made it, so I lay there, my heart hammering, waiting and watching.

It wasn't until after four o'clock that the light snapped off and I saw Roy come out of the bungalow and cross to the cabin.

As I heard him come in, I called to him.

"Don't put on the light," he said at the door. "She'll see it."

I peered in the direction of his voice. It was too dark to see him.

"What happened?"

"She showed me the safe, and she asked me to open it," he said. "I told her it was an old type and I couldn't open it."

I drew in a deep breath of relief.

"Then what happened?"

"She said there must be a way of opening it. She wanted me to blast it open. I said it was too dangerous. I told her dynamite wasn't in my line."

"Did she believe you?"

"Why not? I made it sound pretty convincing."

"Did she say why she wanted it open?"

"Yeah." There was a pause, then he went on, "She said there was money in the safe. If I opened it, we would share it." Another long pause, then he asked, "Is there any money in the safe, Chet?"

I knew it would be fatal to tell him the truth.

"Three hundred dollars," I lied. "Jenson kept it there against an emergency. She's not after that; she's after the confession."

"She said there was a lot of money there."

"She's lying. It was a bait to make you open the safe."

"Yeah . . . well, she'll be disappointed."

The following morning, while Roy was supervising the unloading of gas into our tanks, and I was watching him through the window, I heard my bedroom door creak open.

Lola came in. She closed the door and leaned against it.

It jolted me to see how she had changed.

She had lost weight. Her face was drawn and granite hard. There were dark smudges under her eyes, and she looked ten years older.

She stared at me.

"Tell me how to open the safe," she said. Her voice was harsh and unsteady. "If you don't tell me, I'll call the police and you'll go back to Farnworth."

But she couldn't blackmail me now. I held all the aces.

"Go ahead and call them," I said. "You won't get the money, and I'll tell them where to find your husband. Don't kid yourself they won't believe my word against yours. I'm not the only one with a reputation for violence. When I tell them about Frank Finney, you're going to be in a hell of a jam."

If I had hit her across her face the effect of my words couldn't have been more startling.

She reared back. I heard her breath hiss out through her clenched teeth. Her face sagged. The fear that jumped into her eyes was ugly to see.

"What do you know about Frank?" she demanded, glaring at me.

"I know you murdered him. You're in a trap, and so am I. We're going to spend the rest of our days here whether we like it or not. There's no way out of it. No one is going to open that safe. I've warned Roy about you. Even if he wanted to, he couldn't open it. He doesn't know how to. You've been wasting your time and your talents."

For a long moment she stared at me, her glittering green eyes hating me, then she went out, leaving the door open.

This round was mine, but I wasn't kidding myself. She wouldn't give up that easily. The next round, if I didn't watch out, could be hers.

Nothing happened for two tense and uneasy days, then on the third day after her visit to me Roy told me she was going to a movie in Wentworth.

The red light flashed up in my mind.

"She is going to leave you alone here?" I said, staring at him.

"She's movie mad," he said, shrugging. "She wanted me to go with her, but I told her I wasn't leaving you alone—besides, someone has to run this joint."

"You're not kidding yourself, are you?" I said. "She's not going to the movies. She's baiting the hook for you."

He made an impatient movement.

"I wonder, sometimes, if you're not crazy in the head. What's on your mind now?"

"She's told you there's money in the safe. By now, she knows that money means everything to you. She's gambling on your weakness. She's gambling on the hope that as soon as she is out of the way, you'll open the safe, but she won't have gone far. She'll be back in time to catch you opening the safe. It's her only chance to fool you into opening it."

"I told you, I'm not opening it!"

"Okay, just as long as you remember that when she drives away."

It was a little after ten o'clock when I saw her get into the Mercury. Roy saw her off. He stood in the moonlight, his hands on his hips, watching the tail lights disappear up the mountain road. He stood there for a long time, watching, then he walked over to the lunch room and out of my sight.

I lay there in bed, looking through the window, waiting for something to happen, knowing that something must happen, and feeling instinctively that this was the end of my road.

I could imagine Roy pacing up and down in the kitchen, his shrewd, greedy mind questioning both Lola's and my stories. Was there big money in the safe? Was there a confession in there? Was this a trap to persuade him to open the safe?

Nothing happened for an hour. It was the longest hour I have ever lived through, then I saw the headlights of a truck come down the road. The truck pulled up by the gas pumps.

Roy came out of the lunch room and serviced the truck. He and the trucker talked for a few minutes, then the truck drove away.

This was the moment. I knew it by the way my heart began to thump.

Roy stood by the pumps, looking towards the steep hill that led over the mountain to Wentworth. He stood there for three or four minutes, staring into the darkness. There were no approaching headlights to alarm him.

Then he walked quickly to the bungalow.

This uncontrolled urge for money in him had been too much for him. He was going to open the safe!

I watched him pause before the front door of the bungalow. He had obviously come prepared, for it was only a matter of seconds before he pushed open the door and went inside.

But he was being very cautious.

He reappeared again almost immediately. Again he looked up the long, mountain road to make sure she wasn't returning, then satisfied, he went back into the bungalow.

I saw the light go up in the living-room.

It would take him only a few minutes to open the safe and to find the money. There was nothing I could do about it. I had played my cards. They had been just not good enough.

Then I saw her.

She must have coasted the car down the hill without lights sometime after Roy had gone into the lunch room. She had done it superbly well. Although I had been watching all the time, I hadn't seen her come, nor had I seen her park the car.

But there she was, moving quickly and silently towards the bungalow.

The light of the moon showed her up in her green dress as she crossed a patch of white sand. Then she disappeared into the shadows.

The trap was sprung, and Roy had fallen into it.

I imagined him squatting before the safe. With his knowledge, it wouldn't take him long to open it. The sight of all that money would stun him. It would stun him hard enough not to hear the door open. She would kill him. I was sure of that, and there she was, already within yards of him.

I threw off the sheet and blanket that covered me. I swung my feet to the floor. I got to the door in an unsteady rush and grabbed the handle to support myself.

Pain raged in my chest, but I ignored it. All I could think of was that I had to get to the bungalow and save him.

Somehow I got the door open. I crossed the hall and pulled open the front door.

There was a warm, moist feeling at my chest that told me I was bleeding. That was to be expected, I didn't care.

I opened the front door and moved unsteadily into the darkness. There was now no sign of Lola.

Staggering and slowly, I started across the sand to the bungalow. The wound in my chest had burst open, and I could feel blood running down my stomach and thighs, but I kept on.

I was within reach of the bungalow's front door when I heard the violent, choked bang of a gun.

The sound made my heart turn a somersault. I paused, hearing the sound of a heavy fall.

Then not caring, knowing this was the end of my road, I pushed open the door and walked into the lounge.

Roy stood against the wall, the .45 in his hand. The safe door stood open, showing its contents, neatly stacked on two shelves. Lying at Roy's feet was Lola. There was a blue-black hole in her forehead to show where he had shot her.

No one could get shot in the head like that and live. One quick look at her told me she was dead.

Roy and I stared at each other. His face was yellow-white and glistening with the sweat of fear.

"You were right," he said, his voice a cracked whisper. "If you hadn't warned me, she would have nailed me."

I felt the strength seeping out of me. Somehow I got to a chair and collapsed into it. The flow of blood made a dark stain on my pyjama trousers.

Roy remained motionless, staring down at Lola. He didn't look at me.

"We've got to get out of here," I said. I put my hand on the pad of bandages that covered my wound and pressed against its warm sogginess. "Get the car! We can't talk our way out of this! Take the money! We can still get away with it!"

He turned his head and looked at the neatly stacked rows of money.

"I knocked the gun out of her hand as she came in," he said. "I didn't mean to kill her."

"Get the car! Come on! We've got to get away from here!" Even to me, my voice sounded far away, and the way I was bleeding frightened me.

"Yeah."

He went to the safe and hauled out the money. He jerked the table cloth off the table and bundled the money into it.

"I'm bleeding," I said. "Fix it, Roy, and get me a coat. I'll be okay."

He turned and stared at me. There was an expression on his face I have never seen before. It made him a stranger to me.

"How far do you imagine you'll get? You're finished!" His voice was harsh with his greed. "With this amount of dough, I can begin a new life—the kind of life I've always wanted to live. There's no room in the car for you! Don't look at me like that! Do you imagine you're worth over a hundred thousand bucks? No man is!" He shook the bundle of money at me. "You said the score was even, didn't you? That's what you said! I'm getting out of here!"

Suddenly I didn't care any more. I let him go. After a minute or so I heard a car engine start up. I saw through the window the headlights of the Mercury light up, then the car swung around. It went away fast towards the mountain road that led to Tropica Springs.

I looked at Lola lying at my feet. There was blood on her face and her mouth was drawn down in a snarl of fear. She looked hideous. I wondered how I could ever have fallen for her; how a man like Jenson could ever have fallen for her.

I had to hold onto the arms of the chair to keep myself from falling. Darkness was creeping in on me. Sooner or later, someone would come to Point of No Return and see the light on in the bungalow. Whoever they were would peer in at the window and find us.

If I were dead by then, it wouldn't matter, but if I were alive, and if they could save my life, then there was no future for me. No one would believe I hadn't killed her. When Jenson's body was found, no one would believe I hadn't killed him either.

So I waited, hoping for death.

There was nothing else to hope for.

THE END

THE ERECTION SET by MICKEY SPILLANE

Dogeron Kelly, a walking bomb of a man, suddenly appears in elegant – and not so elegant – New York circles with a suitcase containing a quarter of a million dollars. There are rumours but no-one is certain where he, or the money, came from. It seems he is out to claim his inheritance – or is there something else he is after?

Sharon Cass, for instance, a bright and beautiful girl with some very special gifts for the right man?

Whatever it is, Dog Kelly isn't telling, but his search takes in a baronial old-family manor; the high levels of international illegal traffic; paid mobsters; the rich and the famous. . . .

THE ERECTION SET

Another blockbuster by one of the world's most popular writers.

0 552 09111 1 – 50p

RUSSIAN ROULETTE by JAMES HADLEY CHASE

Three highly efficient Russian exterminators were coming to London. Their target? Callan.

The reason? He'd been sold out by his own country . . . his own section. But more than that, he'd been set up as a sitting duck for the K.G.B. He couldn't get a gun . . . he couldn't get any money . . . and he couldn't get a passport. . . .

For the first time in his life Callan was the hunted not the hunter – the victim not the executioner. And he didn't like it – not one little bit he didn't like it – and if those bloody Ivans thought he was going to make things easy for them, they had another think coming! He was going to fight – and he was going to fight the only way he knew how . . . dirty . . . very dirty. . . .

0 552 09762 4 – 60p

THE WORLD IN MY POCKET by JAMES HADLEY CHASE

The prize was a million-bucks payroll of the Rocket Research Station and some of the most heavily guarded cash in existence. . . .

The red-head started it all. Her name was Ginny. She was hard and bright as a diamond, and she came to Morgan's mob with a scheme for snatching the armoured truck, overpowering the driver and guard, and bursting the time lock. The mob was sceptical. It all sounded too easy – especially coming from a broad. But they'd had enough of working for peanuts, and with two hundred thousand each, they'd have the world in their pockets. . . .

0 552 09820 5 – 40p

MISS SHUMWAY WAVES A WAND by JAMES HADLEY CHASE

How come a New York reporter like Ross Millan was combing half Mexico looking for old man Shumway's missing daughter?

Millan had asked himself the question a dozen times – and when he found her, he asked himself a whole lot more questions. For the shapely blonde he'd seen in the photograph turned out to be a fast-talking lady who packed a punch like a prize fighter, did a little magic on the side, and just happened to be a dip – a very efficient pickpocket. From the day little Miss Myra Shumway walked into Millan's life, things were never quite the same. . . .

0 552 10381 0 – 65p

A SELECTED LIST OF CRIME STORIES
FOR YOUR READING PLEASURES

All these books are available at your bookshop or newsagent, or can be ordered direct from the publisher. Just tick the titles you want and fill in the form below.

CORGI BOOKS, Cash Sales Department, P.O. Box 11, Falmouth, Cornwall.

Please send cheque or postal order, no currency.

U.K. send 19p for first book plus 9p per copy for each additional book ordered to a maximum charge of 73p to cover the cost of postage and packing.

B.F.P.O. and Eire allow 19p for first book plus 9p per copy for the next 6 books, thereafter 3p per book.

Overseas Customers. Please allow 20p for the first book and 10p per copy for each additional book.

NAME (block letters) ....

ADDRESS ....

(DEC 77) ....